HellBound Books
Anthology of
Creature Features

curated by

Samantha Hawkins

A HellBound Books® LLC Publication

Copyright © 2025 by HellBound Books® Publishing LLC
All Rights Reserved

Cover design by Tee Arts for
HellBound Books® Publishing LLC

www.hellboundbookspublishing.com

No part of this publication can be reproduced, stored in a retrieval system, or transmitted by any form or by any means, mechanical, digital, electronic, photocopying or recording, except for inclusion in a review, without permission in writing from the individual contributors and the publisher.
All contents in this anthology are works of fiction. Names, characters, places and incidents are imaginary. Any resemblance to actual persons, places, or occurrences are coincidental only.

Contents:

The Goldfish
Tim Newton Anderson

Dad said it was cruel to give goldfish as prizes, but Brian said he was the one who hooked the duck, and he should be able to choose whatever he wanted.

"That's stupid," his Dad said. "You should have a proper prize. They buy these things half-dead already. It won't last as far as home. I've spent a fortune in this place. The least they could do is give you something worth winning."

But Brian insisted.

They had only recently moved to Great Witcherley in the Norfolk Fens, and this was the first time they had visited Wishlock's Circus on its annual visit. Dad rushed him past the sideshows advertising unusual creatures and did not let go of his hand until they had reached the fairground. Some of the sideshows had been intriguing: a mermaid, a fortune teller who was supposed to be an immortal wizard. But his dad told Brian he was too small to see them just yet. Give it a couple of years.

Brian had been on the big Ferris wheel—well, big by Great Witcherley's standards although a lot smaller than the one they'd seen on a visit to London—and the carousel. His dad had offered a ride on the teacups, but Brian said he was too old for them. He was eight on his next birthday. He wanted to visit the Big Top, but his dad said they should get the goldfish home before it died, and they could come back the next day. The circus was there all week before it went off to wherever it stayed for the winter.

The goldfish still looked fine when they got home, as Brian had said it would be. He'd wanted to get one of those round bowls he'd seen on the television, but his dad said they might as well just put it in with his own fish in the big tank in the living room. That fish tank was one of the reasons Brian had been so insistent on getting the goldfish. It was his dad's pride and joy with exotic, multi-coloured fish he had been buying for as long as Brian could remember. He'd been dragged to the pet shop at the Garden Centre where they used to live every Saturday and spent hours talking to the staff about what could live with what and the best way to look after them. Dad had bought all sort of equipment to keep them happy and filled the bottom with treasure chests, plastic rocks, and a toy man in a diving suit who would go up and down as air bubbled through a pipe in his helmet. There were special plants, too.

Mum said it was a waste of money. They didn't do anything interesting and cost a small fortune. Not to mention the top-of-the-range food. But Dad said watching them was the only thing keeping him calm, what with his stressful job and the regular arguments with Mum. Those had become more frequent and louder since he'd been forced to move away from his friends and family to what he called 'the middle of nowhere' when the firm he worked for had been taken over.

When Dad cleaned the tank, he took the fish out carefully in a special net and moved them to his back-up tank which he kept in the cupboard under the stairs. But he just dumped the goldfish in straight from its plastic bag.

Brian thought that was rude and he said so, earning him a clip on the back of the head. Those had gotten more frequent too, recently, along with being sent to bed early most nights without a glass of water or a bedtime story. Dad wasn't the only one to suffer from the move. Brian was taken away from the school and friends he loved, and his new class was full of children who were all related and looked like each other and only spoke to him to call him names. At least, now that he had the goldfish, he had a friend who was all his own.

He pulled his small chair over to the fish tank after supper and watched his fish swim round with the others as Mum and Dad watched the telly. Dad's fish were more exotic with their bright neon colours and fancy fins and tails. But his goldfish was their king.

Mum and Dad weren't shouting tonight, just snapping at each other about what to watch and who should have the remote control. Dad reckoned Mum couldn't use it properly or was deliberately missing bits of his favourite programme as she fast forwarded past the adverts. Dad was right, watching the fish did reduce Brian's sense of anxiety at the likely explosion of their grumbling into a full-scale row. He didn't even mind when he was sent off to bed because he could look forward to seeing his fish again in the morning.

As he lay in bed, the voices of his parents grew louder as the blazing argument he'd feared erupted into life. To block the noise out, he imagined he was a fish swimming with his goldfish in the tank. Mum had taught him to swim when he was only three, and he loved the cool water on his skin as he slipped through the water. That was another thing he missed in their new home. There was no pool nearby, and his parents said he was too young to swim in the river like the other children.

His new fishy friend showed him lots of acrobatic swimming tricks; spinning in different directions as it sped from one end of the tank to the other. He found he could do them too, and the two of them invented all kinds of aquatic dances which impressed Dad's fish. They tapped their fins against their sides in a sort of applause. Brian and the goldfish, which he'd named Gerald, were stars. He was smiling as he slipped off to sleep, dreaming of the fun he and his new friend were having.

The next day was Monday, and Brian and his father were in a bit of a mood. Neither was looking forward to their day—Brian at school and his dad at work. Dad's mood was even worse when he looked at the fish tank and saw one of his favourites floating dead on the surface.

"That flaming goldfish has killed my Discus Fish," he shouted. "That cost me £50."

"What?" said Mum. "You told me it was only £10."

This stopped Dad's rant for a few seconds and gave Brian a chance to chip in.

"It's not my goldfish's fault," he said. "It's a friendly fish. It's my friend. Your stupid fish was probably just sick with something."

Dad wanted to continue with the argument but realised if he did, he would be late for work. He often complained his boss was out to get rid of him, and he couldn't afford to give him an excuse, so he grabbed his briefcase and stomped out of the door, slamming it behind him.

"And you can shut up as well," Mum said. "It's not your friend; it's just another stupid fish."

She walked over to the tank and put her fingers in the water. Gerald darted to the top and nudged her hand.

"Ow," she shouted, pulling her hand away. "It bit me."

"It can't have," said Brian. "Fish don't have teeth."

"Piranhas do," she said, sucking her fingers. "I've seen them on telly. Strip all the flesh off your bones. That fish goes as soon as your dad gets home."

"No, please, Mum," said Brian. Now he had something else to worry about. As well as being scared the other kids would call him names again, he had the threat of Dad's anger and punishment hanging over him. "I promise I'll be good if you let my fish alone."

Mum threw his bag with his lunch across the room, and he only just managed to catch it. If he hadn't, that would be another reason to be punished.

If he thought telling the class he had a pet would make them like him, he was wrong.

"Brian's got a fishy friend," said Dave, the largest of his classmates and the one the others all followed. "He should have his fishy on a little dishy. You eat fish, you idiot, you don't make friends with them. Brian's got fishy fingers. Fishy, fishy Brian."

The others all joined in. "Fishy, fishy Brian."

The teacher, Miss Williams, came into the class and told them to stop, but she didn't try and comfort Brian as he cried silent tears in the corner. She was from Great Witcherley, too, and was related to most of their parents. No one in the village liked the newcomers who lived on the new estate at its edge. Perhaps in fifty years they may accept them, but for now, they were incomers who didn't know their traditions and generally made no effort to do so.

As soon as the morning lessons were over and they were marshalled across to the dining hall to eat their lunch, the chants started again.

"Fishy, fishy Brian. Have you brought your friend to eat today? Fishy on a little dishy. Yum, yum, yum."

The tears came back, and he ran outside, leaving his uneaten lunch and bag on the table.

It would mean yet another row, but he couldn't face going back into the school. It was only a few minutes' walk to the wood on the edge of the village, and he stumbled in until he found a clearing where he sat on a fallen tree and let the tears flow. In a few seconds, he was crying with deep gulps of air shaking his small body. He could hardly breathe as all his pain and fear tore at his stomach and chest and clamped across his shoulders like giant hands. He'd always tried to keep it inside. When he did cry, it just made his parents' anger worse. Dad would call him a cry-baby and give him another slap for daring to show his emotions. He wished his goldfish had legs, so the two of them could run away together. Back home to London where he might be taken in by an aunt and uncle, or the parents of his old friends.

The sobs had subsided somewhat when he heard a noise behind him and turned to see an old man. He must be local as he had the typical red hair and bushy beard of Great Witchingham, although his were threaded with grey.

"How do, bor," he said. "What you doin' out of school?"

Brian had been brought up not to talk to strangers, especially not to tell them why you might be upset if it had anything to do with what happened at home. But the words came tumbling out as freely as his tears.

"Nobody likes me, they call me Fishy Brian, and when I get home, my dad might kill my fish, and it's my only friend, and I'm scared to go to school, and scared to go home, and I don't know what to do."

The old man crouched next to Brian and placed his bag on the ground. It had fallen open, showing a dead rabbit inside.

"That's what you call a dilemma," the man said. "Ain't there nothin you can do? Seems like you need to talk to your folks and tell them how much this here fish means to you."

"It's not like its special like Dad's fish. It's only a goldfish from the fair," said Brian. "But it's the first pet I've ever had, and I love it, and I don't believe it killed one of Dad's fish. It must just have died."

"Are you sure it's not special?" the man asked. "Lots of special fish round here: Grandfather Trout, Mocha Derek the silver pike. Mebbe this here goldfish of yours is one of those magic ones. The fair's special so it makes sense they'd give away special goldfish. You tell your ma and pa that, and mebbe they'll let you keep em."

"They'll still be mad I bunked school," Brian said.

"You just tell em you're sick, see," the man answered. "Go home now. You'm lookin' pale enough anyways. Chances are they won't kill a sick child's goldfish. Tell you what, I've got a magic stone in my bag. I wishes on it, and it makes sure there's lots of rabbits for me to catch. See, it's got a hole in it. Look through, and it'll grant your heart's desire."

"Don't you need it?" Brian asked.

"Nice of you to worry about me," the man said. "Shows what a good un you are. Reckon as how I can find another one, and anyways I've got plenty of rabbits for today's supper, and tomorrow as well. Reckon you need it more than me."

He handed Brian a grey stone that was smooth and warm in the palm of his hand. He was tempted to lift it up and look through the hole, but he thought he'd better keep it for when he really needed it. He didn't know how many times the magic would work.

The man started to walk away. Brian was startled by a noise on the opposite side of the clearing and turned to see what it was. When he looked back, the man had gone. Back at home, he wished he'd used the stone. There was no sympathy from his mother for his supposed illness. The school had called and told her he'd left without saying anything or taking his bag. He was sent to bed as a punishment, not to get better.

Things were even worse when his father came home. Normally he received a slap on the leg or a clip round the head when his father was angry, but this time, he was punched hard in the stomach and slapped across the face, leaving a bright red mark that didn't fade for several hours. When it did, there was a dark blue bruise.

Even worse than the assault, his father went over to the fish tank and lifted out his goldfish by the tail. Gerald looked like he was trying to fight back, twisting upwards as if he could bite his hand, but Dad just stamped to the toilet and flushed the fish down the pan. Brian had stifled his tears when he was being hit, but the sight of Gerald swirling away into the drains brought the sobbing back. His cheeks were soaked as he was marched back to bed with no supper.

"You've been impossible since you got that stupid fish," his father said. "You would never have dared talk back to me or bunk off school before you got the goldfish. Bad enough I have to deal with a job I hate and your stupid mother in this backwards village of inbred mutants, without you being an even bigger pain in the butt than normal."

As usual, Mum said nothing, happy to have her husband's anger directed somewhere other than at her.

From the shouts and sounds of things being thrown he heard from his bedroom, that hadn't worked. However, she gave as much as she got.

As soon as his crying stopped long enough for him to breathe freely, he pulled the stone out of his pocket. He looked through the hole, which was pointing towards the bedroom window. He could clearly see the stars in the sky in the patterns which he knew were supposed to mean something but which no one had ever taken the time to explain to him.

"They should all suffer the way they make me suffer," he said. "The bullies, my mum and dad, everyone. I miss my fish. I want Gerald back safely at home."

He wasn't sure if there was a proper formula for making a wish on the stone, but he hoped the magic would pick up on what he meant. If he was honest, just getting his fish back would be enough. With Gerald safe in the tank, he could cope with everything else.

He was pleased to see Dad had already left for work when he came down for breakfast, already dressed in his school uniform. He didn't want to risk getting his mum mad again. Thankfully, she was in a quiet mood, subdued you could call her, possibly because of the bruise that was on her cheek and the way she was holding her ribs protectively. Apart from warning him not to skip school again, he left home without a row.

He was dawdling a bit to delay getting to school as long as possible but was surprised to see most of his classmates gathered in a huddle by the river. He was sure he hadn't missed a note about some kind of out of school activity but went over to join them. Instead of the excitement he would've expected at getting out of the classroom for a few hours, they were all quiet with drawn faces. They didn't even acknowledge his presence, much less call him names, as he pushed his way through them to see what they were looking at.

They were all standing behind some stripy tape that had been strung between metal poles with 'POLICE DO NOT CROSS' written on it. The police were on the other side, gathered around a body that looked as if it had been pulled out of the river. At first Brian couldn't see much as the officers obscured his view. Then one of them moved away.

It was a boy a bit bigger than him. It was Dave, the chief bully. Brian's first guess was that he must have fallen in and drowned. Mum was always saying the river was dangerous because a freak current could drag you under or you could get snagged in a tree root or some other object hidden by the water. But if Dave had drowned, that wasn't all that killed him. Even though the water had washed away the blood and turned his flesh grey, Dave had had his throat ripped open. There were clear teeth marks, although quite small ones, around the open wound.

It was too much for Brian, and he pushed his way to the back of the group of schoolchildren and noisily threw up in some bushes. As he wiped his mouth on the sleeve of his jacket, he noticed he wasn't the first person to have vomited there.

He was pulling himself together when Miss Williams arrived and shepherded them to school. One of Dave's close friends, Billy, told Brian that Dave had gone to the river for an early morning swim when whatever happened, happened. Their common grief over their friend's death seemed to make them accept Brian as part of the group. Brian was wise enough not to say what he felt - relief and pleasure at the death of the bully, who'd led the campaign against him. However horrible Dave's death sounded to be, he was happy about it but managed to act sad rather than wearing the grin he felt inside. No one mentioned 'Fishy, fishy Brian'.

There were lots of theories the other boys came up with. He'd been grabbed by a pervert and held under water after he tried to fight the man off. He'd simply got a cramp and drowned. There was some kind of monster—a giant eel, a mermaid, or a crocodile that had escaped from a zoo—that had grabbed him and bit his throat out. Miss Williams clamped down on their gossip in the classroom, but it burst into life when they went out at break and lunch times. Brian had his own speculation. The bite marks looked familiar, and he remembered the mark on his mother's finger. The thought was exciting.

The Headmaster had come into their classroom to say he was arranging for a counsellor to visit them, but they all agreed they didn't need someone to talk to. They needed answers. In the countryside, death was a fact of life, and most of them had seen their parents kill farm animals. They'd also all seen their elderly relatives die— as they tended to breathe their last at home rather than a hospital—and quite a few knew people who'd been killed in farming accidents. What was different about Dave's death was the strange nature of those bite marks, and how such a strong swimmer could drown. Brian didn't share his speculation.

He allowed the smile he'd been hiding all day to light up his face as he walked home. It faltered a little when he turned the corner into his cul-de-sac and saw a police car outside his door. A female police officer was standing at the side door, and she came over to him.

"What's happened?" he asked.

There was a cold sharp stab in his stomach. Had his dad done something to his mum? Or her to him? Neither would surprise him.

What did surprise him was that his Uncle Ian and Aunt Sandra were standing in the kitchen. Uncle Ian was his mum's brother, and Brian had met them a few times on the rare occasions they'd been to family events. Mum had sometimes suggested they could come to visit, but Dad didn't really like her seeing her family.

"Come into the living room, Brian," said Aunt Sandra. "The police want to know when you last saw your parents. They seem to have gone missing. Your dad didn't turn up for work, and when someone from his office came round to pick up some papers, they found the door open and no one at home."

Brian didn't know what he should be feeling. Then he looked over at the fish tank, and that broad smile he had earlier burst across his face. His goldfish was back in there.

He should go into the living room with his relatives and the police, but he couldn't help running over to the tank. Gerald was swimming around happily as if he'd never left, weaving in and out of the fronds of the plants, nudging the diver, and swooping down towards the treasure chest with its plastic gold that matched the colour of his scales.

He didn't notice the other fish in the tank at first. Seven of them were floating at the top of the tank, dead—all of his father's collection. There were still two other fish in the tank, but Brian had never seen them. One was black; the colour of his hair. And his father's. And the other was the brown of his mother's hair and had a purple mark on its cheek. It was no wonder Brian hadn't seen them at first as they seemed to be cowering in a corner of the tank, while Gerald swam majestically up and down.

"Don't worry, Brian," said Uncle Ian. "If you want to bring your fish with you when you come to our house, you can. The police have agreed you can stay with us until they find where your parents are."

Great, I can relax. Brian took Aunt Sandra's hand and let himself be led into the living room where he was given a sandwich to eat and a glass of cola to drink. The lady police officer asked a few questions. As soon as they realised he knew nothing about his parent's disappearance, Uncle Ian said Brian should go upstairs and get some clothes, and he would find some kind of bowl they could bring the fish in. They would bring the tank on a separate trip or buy one from a shop near where they lived back in Brian's hometown.

When they down with Brian's bag packed, he went back over to the fish tank. There were now nine dead fish on the surface with only Gerald still alive.

"What's happened here?" asked Uncle Ian.

"It's all right," said Brian. "Gerald the Goldfish is the only one that's mine. The rest were Dad's."

"I wonder if someone put something in the water," said the lady police officer. "I'll have it checked. Better get fresh water if you're taking the goldfish. Lucky it seems to be okay, Brian. Must be really tough. I'm sure you are tough as well and will be all right with your aunt and uncle until we find your parents."

I will. And you don't need to rush.

"Can we bury the others?" Brian asked. The PC nodded. "I think a sort of burial at sea would be best."

He got a sieve from under the sink and scooped them all up from the top. He carried them, dripping, to the downstairs loo, emptied them in, and pressed the flush lever.

"Bye, bye," he said. What he left unsaid was 'good riddance'. As he walked into the kitchen to start his new life, he fingered the stone in his pocket and smiled.

Fingers
R. D. Tyler

The dog is licking my fingers again.

Every night, I drop my arm off the edge of the bed and let it dangle. And every night, Lucy licks my fingers from under the bed. It drives me nuts, but I keep encouraging her by putting my arm down for her. I should probably train her to stop, but it's become kinda comforting. It's like that annoying habit from your favorite friend. You hate it, but if they ever stop, a core bit of them goes missing. The unique quirks and annoyances are what make it love.

Her tongue scrapes between each finger. She goes and goes, slurping away at whatever it is on my hand she can't get enough of, until my arm goes numb, and I pull it away. Her slobber leaves a sticky residue, but I'm too tired to wipe it off.

She's been doing it since the first night she came home from the shelter as a puppy. The shelter people told me Lucy was a boxer-pit bull mix, and it was love at first sight. She was a tiny, timid thing, shivering in my lap the whole way home. As soon as I set her down, she scurried under the bed. Her golden eyes peered out from the shadows, taking in everything in this unfamiliar setting. I put her bedding in the corner with some treats to coax her out, but she stayed put.

Giving her time to adjust, I went to lie down. I've always been an edge sleeper. I like to lie with my body as close to the edge of the bed as I can, usually hanging a leg or an arm off. It's just what feels right to me. I don't feel comfortable in the middle of the bed. I don't know what that says about me. I was drifting away with my arm drooped like normal when there was this tiny wetness on the palm of my hand.

I scooched my head enough to peek over and see this black, nose on a brown, face licking my hand, content as could be. My heart melted. The rascal had dragged her bedding under the bed and was lying half on it, her front paws hanging off the side, and her neck stretched so she could reach my hand.

And that was our first night together.

And every night ever since, for four years. Lucy's grown into a big dog now, almost a full sixty pounds. She barely fits under the bed anymore. Her puppy brown coat developed into a light brindle pattern with a small white stripe on her wide nose. She has an underbite and goofy, pendulous cheeks that wobble ever so slightly when she tilts her head at me.

I roll over to my back and let my other arm drop over the edge. She starts licking those fingers.

"Ugh, I can hear your spit sloshing," I tell her.

She doesn't stop. I close my eyes, trying to let the drowsiness win. She still doesn't stop.

"You need a bath, you reek." I thought she'd react to that, but she just keeps going. She hates baths, even hates the word, but she gets that nasty, waxy smell too easily. It doesn't smell like that, but with each slurp of her tongue, a wave of something pours out and burns my nostrils. Something rotten.

Maybe she got into the trash earlier? I'm finally starting to fade. She's always eating something she shouldn't. Both my arms are asleep now, the one dangling off the edge and the one resting on my chest. My hands are numb, tingly. Sleep almost has me.

There's a heavy bounce on the mattress and absentmindedly I go to pet Lucy. She doesn't get on the bed often. I don't mind either way. She's such a good cuddle buddy. I scratch behind her floppy ears. She's whining beside me, nuzzling me frantically. I wrap my arm around her, shaking her a bit with the hug.

"What is it, girl?"

She's still licking my fingers under the bed.

I bolt up in a panic, jerking my hand away. Lucy can't be in two places at once. I clearly see her on the bed. I don't have two dogs.

I notice my hand. The one that until a moment ago had been under the bed being licked by something. I can't feel it at all, but it's all raw and bloody. My first two fingers are nothing but shredded meat and exposed bone. The other two are rubbed raw enough that the skin is split. I'm bleeding all over the sheets.

I scream.

"What the fuck?" They're the first words that come to mind when I finish screaming.

I can't think straight. Panting comes from under the bed. It sounds like Lucy's but wrong. Slower, maybe a bit deeper. Hungrier. Lucy is shaking on the bed. Her hackles are up. Her whine goes up and up in pitch until dropping into a growl. The whites of her eyes are visible as she stares back and forth between me and the edge of the bed.

I tuck my legs up close and center my body in the middle of the mattress. I awkwardly rip off a pillowcase and try to wrap my bleeding hand. It's my left hand. I'm left-handed. I'm shaking, stressed out of my mind, and my right hand doesn't seem to want to work. It takes a few tries before I can get the makeshift bandage to stay put. Blood seeps through before I'm even finished tying it. I tuck my wrapped-up hand in my right armpit and squeeze as tight as I can.

It doesn't hurt. Why doesn't it hurt? I look at my right hand. It's still a little numb but the feeling is slowly coming back. I work my fingers back and forth. They are raw too, but they're not bleeding at least.

A scuttling from under the bed snaps my focus back. What the fuck is under my bed? Lucy is frantic now. She barks, each bark echoing throughout the bedroom. The scuttling stops, then sounds again, like it has retreated farther under the bed.

Directly under me.

Fuck.

The springs of the box-spring twang. Something is pulling on them, pushing through them. There's a pressure under me. I shift away from it. A bulge rises in the middle of the mattress where I had just been sitting as whatever it is tries to force its way up through the bed.

Fuck fuck fuck fuck fuck.

I punch the lump without thinking. At least I'm subconsciously aware enough to use my right hand. I hit again. And again. As hard as I can. There's an almost imperceptible squeal, and the bulge recedes. Lucy's barks are still resounding right in my ear.

"Lucy, shut up! Please shut up, shut up," My heart is exploding, and there's a pulsing in my wrapped hand that matches my heart. I grab her into a hug to try to get her to quiet down. I don't know what to do, and the barking is making it worse.

There's a click-clack of something hitting the wood of the floor, then a small splash like something large submerging in water. Am I dreaming? Is this a nightmare, and there's some nightmare bug in a lake under my bed that ate my fingers? Am I going to wake up soon?

Searing pain shoots through my left hand and tells me, no, I'm not waking up soon. This is fucking real. Whatever had stopped the pain finally wears off, and it all came back at once. I cradle my hand and rock back and forth, sucking in air, just trying to breathe through the burning.

Lucy finally stops barking. She's just whimpering now. Under the bed, it's silent. No clicking, no breathing. There is stillness. I can't tell if it's it' is there anymore or not.

I have a flashlight on the nightstand. There is a baseball bat in the corner of the room. I squeeze Lucy for courage, then as carefully as I can, I reach over to the nightstand, trying not to disturb the mattress. Just as I wrap my fingers around the light, the frame squeaks.

I coil my legs and explode off the bed, trying to reach the far wall with my leap. I clear most of the room, hitting the ground with a heavy thud. I catch myself with my forearms on the closet door and the wall that forms the corner where the bat sits. The closet door rattles against my weight. The bed rattles behind me in answer. I stare into the corner, my neck frozen. I'm too scared to turn around, to even move my eyes to one side or the other. My hand throbs.

I take a quick breath to steady myself, then click on the flashlight and stick it in my mouth. I grab the baseball bat high up on the handle to give me better leverage. Less power, but more control. Scraping along the side of the wall, I inch toward the light switch on the other side of the room.

After what feels like hours, I reach the switch. I flick it up. For a second, the light doesn't come on, and panic rises in me, but finally after a mini eternity, the bulb shines and fills the room. I risk a look at the bed.

Lucy is still on the bed, dancing back and forth on her paws. It's her 'I need to go outside' dance, but on cocaine. Her eyes are wild, her boxer face flinging drool everywhere. Under the bed is shadow and darkness, and I can't see anything.

I debate for a moment what to do. My phone is charging downstairs. I could run out, call for medical attention and come back with help. Hopefully help with guns and flamethrowers. But I couldn't leave Lucy. What if it goes after her? I'm not going to sacrifice her to escape.

Maybe I should look to see what's under the bed so I can confirm there really is something down there. It could just be a fucked-up raccoon that got in. Yeah. Just a fucked-up raccoon.

Lucy whimpers just as more pain seared through my hand. Medical attention is the priority, but I'd get Lucy to come with me. I took a small step forward, closer to the bed. Then another. One more. A shudder came from under the bed . Close enough.

"Come on, girl. Come here," I beckon her with the bat. I pat my chest with my left forearm. The white pillowcase is now a red so dark it's almost black. I think the bleeding has stopped though. She looks askance at me, takes a step forward, then stops.

"Please Lucy. You gotta jump! Come here! Let's get treats!" I coax and plead with her.

She's too scared to jump and I'm too scared to grab her. Coward's standoff. Please, you goddamn dog, come here.

Finally, she jumps off the bed. I wish she'd jumped to me. She lands halfway between me and the bed.

Something moves fast from under the bed. It's a blur but something like a big black hook swipes at Lucy's hindquarters. It slices into her, sending her back legs flying. Lucy yelps as she tumbles. I rush to her, and she gets back up and lunges at me. I wrap my arms around her and throw us both back toward the door. We slam against it, and it knocks the wind out of me. The bed shakes furiously.

In the commotion, I dropped the light, and now it rolls on the floor. As it settles, the beam points under the bed. I'm already on my side, so I tilt my head to get a better view. I lose what little breath I'd gotten back.

What seems to be a miniature lake replaces the floor underneath my bed, ripples on its surface radiating out from the center. The surface is dark, but what I can only describe as stars reflect, blinking in and out. It gives off a faint bluish, purplish glow. In the middle of the star-lake under my bed, half submerged is a face.

The face is like a cross between a cat and a crocodile. It has a long, rounded snout but with whiskers and a feline nose. Its eyes are somehow both too far apart and too close together to look quite natural and are sickly yellow with black slits. Its skin is dark and scaly with coarse hairs sticking everywhere. It reminds me of the closeups I've seen of insects and spiders. Chitinous. That's a good word to describe it.

As I stare at it, it stares back at me. The face shudders and opens its mouth, letting out something in between a hiss and a guttural groan. The inside of its mouth isn't pink but a horrid reddish-brown. It has rows of countless flaps of flesh, hundreds of translucent uvulas where the teeth should be. Globs of thick, mucusy saliva drips from those flaps. It sticks out its tongue, and the tongue starts to vibrate. It's too long and thin, like a frog's tongue, but covered in thousands of small spines. It ends with a pair of small pincers.

I want to vomit.

The creature begins bobbing up and down, partially rising in and out of the lake-portal thing. The portal ripples but doesn't splash. The bobbing reminds me of a daddy longlegs or a lizard when they bounce when they feel threatened. You feel threatened, you eldritch horror looking fuck? I wasn't the one munching on your space tentacles.

It doesn't seem to want to come out from under the bed but doesn't want to go all the way back through the portal either. Maybe it doesn't like the light.

Lucy's whimper takes my attention off the thing under my bed. I check her leg. It's not a deep cut but thick ooze is coming out of it, almost more of that than blood. I press my bandaged hand against it, briefly wondering about dog-to-human bloodborne diseases. I try to wipe the ichor out. She yelps when I touch it.

I glance at the bed. The thing's still bobbing up and down, faster now, but it hasn't moved any closer.

I reach for the doorknob, watching the creature, seeing how it would react. Its frog-cat-mosquito tongue begins whipping around its snout, hitting itself, flinging drops of saliva everywhere. I grip the knob. Ever so slowly, I start twisting it. The tongue spins, lashing ever more wildly. The latch releases. There's a vile retching, and before I can open the door, purplish slime flies in a wad at the door handle, coating my arm, the knob, and a good part of the door. I lose feeling in my hand, again. Between the slime and the numbness, I lose traction, and my fingers slides off the handle.

There's a scuttling noise behind me. I have a split second to either try the door again or dodge out of the way. Instinct serves me well. I roll, Lucy and bat cradled in my arms, a lopsided ball that barely makes it out of the way as the creature charges from under the bed and slams into the door.

It has an arachnid-like body, just a giant hairy bulb. It's big enough around—if I were to hug it, my fingertips would only just touch. Not that I want to hug this thing. It has eight long, spindly legs, four on each side, but two of those pairs point in the wrong direction. They point up. The feet are two-toed arthropod claws. Thick, coarse hair dots each leg sporadically.

Hanging from its ass is a thin, segmented, scorpion-like tail, but instead of curling up over its body, it curls under. The tail terminates not in a stinger, but in a pair of boneless 'hands' with limp, flaccid fingers. Each finger flops around as the hands rub themselves like a nervous pervert. It disturbs me, deeply.

I scream, already hoarse, and swing with the bat with all the force I can muster. I'm on my side, my hand's still numb, so it's not a lot of force, but I connect with one of the legs. It's still enough to crumple the leg and spider-scorpion-crocodile-cat beast from hell whimpers and drops. Its upside-down reverse legs extend to cling to the ceiling, catching itself before it could fully collapse. It pulls its body up. Its bottom three legs spasm angrily. At least the one I whacked dangles weakly.

The tongue shoots out and wraps itself around my foot. Before I can brace myself, I'm yanked up by my leg and dragged toward its mouth. I lose hold of the bat, and it clatters to the flood. For just a moment, all those dangly bits gum my foot and leg, then all feeling is gone. The revulsion remains.

I squirm and twist. The monster's bottom-pointed legs grope at me, trying to pin me still. The 'hands' of the tail slap at me limply, which bothers me more. I wrestle with all the limbs as best I can, but I know I'm not going to make it.

I kick out with my free foot, hitting one of those yellow eyes more from luck than aim. It blinks at me. and from around my trapped foot there's an angry growl. I keep kicking. The beast shakes. and pain shoots up my leg.

White crumbs rain down us both. The ceiling drywall can't hold both our weights and cracks where the monster's feet cling to it. We crash to the floor, its legs splayed in every direction. My leg is still stuck in its maw.

Lucy throws herself at the thing, all teeth,. paws,. and fury. She bites and scratches, tearing at the creature's sides. There's some slack around my foot as the thing recoils from Lucy's attacks. I plant my other foot on its body and tug, my muscles seizing from exertion. My leg slowly slides out from that slimy mouth. With a final loud squelch, my foot wrenches free.

What's left of my foot at least. All the meat and tissue had been sucked off to above the ankle. Above that, the flesh bubbles and blisters as if it had just been dissolved in acid. The whole of my lower leg is covered in a million tiny hickeys. All my foot bones are exposed. They don't look like they do in Halloween decorations at all.

I vomit. I vomit again. I'm dizzy. I can barely focus. My head feels so heavy, and it's wobbling. I can't keep upright. I'm going to die, and this alien is going to suck off all the meat from my bones like a fucking popsicle.

Not today.

I shake my head. Grab the bat as tight as I can and swing. I swing for its head. I swing again. Again. The creature's front top two legs try to shield it from my blows, but the legs are thin and give way quickly. I hit it in the snout. Then the eye. The top of the head. Its skin cracks rather than bruises. It must be some sort of a shell.

Even being injured and weak, my hits are still hard enough to create dents in its skin-shell. It tries to crawl away, back under the bed. Probably trying to get back to its portal. Fuck that.

Lucy has left gashes all along its side and now clamps her jaws onto the tail. It struggles to shake her off, but she holds tight. Black ichor is oozing out from all over its body. Even with Lucy latched on, the creature is almost to the bed. The back two legs reach the edge of the portal. That seems to give it purchase or strength. It heaves itself faster toward the gate.

I'm sitting on my butt, inching my way toward it, hitting it as best as I can. Its tongue shoots out again and wraps around the bat. I cling to it and throw my weight backwards as it yanks the tongue back into its freakish mouth. We play tug-of-war for a few seconds.

The bat starts to slip from my grasp. Without thinking about it, or I wouldn't have done it, I grab the tongue with my right hand, squeeze and twist. The feeling must be coming back because a hundred little jabs from the spines stab me. A rattling scream tells me the thing doesn't like this much. I wrench my arm back, twist my upper body and do my best to rip the hateful appendage out.

The creature releases the bat, and I fly backwards. The beast's almost to the edge of the pool. Lucy hasn't let go. A few more inches, and Lucy will go under, and it will take her with it. No!

I post myself on the bat, awkwardly getting to one foot. I purposefully don't look at the other one. I throw myself forward, and stab down with the tip of the bat. There's a moment of resistance and then the makeshift stake pierces through the skin of the creature's body, right behind the head. The bat slides in and down as all my weight falls on it. Black-blue slime seeps from the wound, and the monstrosity lets out a screech.

I slam it again, again, and again. The slime drenches me.

The demon space-bug spasms, its legs thrashing and twitching as it tries to get free from the bat and back to the safety of whatever lies under the ocean under my bed. I scream to Lucy, "Lucy! Drop it! Let go!"

It takes her a moment to stop ripping her head side to side. The tail is mangled. She finally lets go. I think she senses the danger from the swirling vortex and steps away, out from under the bed. She returns to my side, standing on guard and alert, almost daring the creature to attack again.

The creature collapses with an exhale. I use the bat as a prod and push the still twitching body toward the pool. *Get this thing out of here*. It drops into the star-lake but there's no splash. It just floats. The fluids leaking from the creature stains the 'water.' It bobs and rotates for a moment longer before it starts to sink lifelessly into whatever abyss it came from.

The tail sticks up out of the portal as it sinks. Right before those boneless hands reach the surface, the surface ripples from the edge to the center. I watch dumbfounded as the portal shrinks in with each ripple, the star-lake under my bed receding and turning back into a wooden floor. The portal closes just before the fingers can go back in, cutting them off and leaving them to lie there, the only evidence the creature was ever here.

Well, the only evidence under the bed. What's left of my leg has started bleeding now. My hands are in agony. Lucy looks covered in blood, filth, and gore, and I have no idea how much of it is hers and how much isn't. The room's destroyed.

I snatch a belt from my dresser and wrap it high on my thigh. I cinch it as down, pinching skin as it constricts. Slip the hook of a discarded hanger under the belt and twist, tightening it into a tourniquet. Using the bat as a cane, I limp downstairs and dial 9-1-1.

"There's…been an…accident. Bleeding. Dog hurt. Help." I think I mutter my address. Not sure. Hopefully I did.

I lie on the floor. I'm so tired. I can't tell if I'm fading into sleep or death. There's a sound next to me. Can't make it out. A whine? Maybe it's Lucy. I feel something wet.

The dog is licking my fingers again.

Annabelle's Dad
Chad Barger

Annabelle woke up to the noise of dad's clunky boots tromping down the hardwood hallway floor. Then he appeared in her doorway, naked, and carrying his shotgun.

The Charlie boys must be back again.

She couldn't stop her gaze from lingering at the fuzzy mess at his groin—the scraggly auburn patch and the chubby turtle head that drooped a little. It wasn't right for an eleven-year-old girl to see her dad's 'thing,' but she was used to it now. It was common. As common as the strawberry freckles on his broad back and the gnarly divot under his arm where the doctors took out the grenade pieces in the war. Besides, he didn't mean for her to see it. He had an oogie head now, wonky brains. At least it wasn't hard this time, looking up at her and twitching.

He paused and wobbled a bit as he shifted his weight from one foot to the other. She sat up and pulled Tay Tay Bear to her chest. Dad's eyes beamed at her. Then he lifted his index finger to his mouth and gave her a silent and intense 'shhhhh' with raised eyebrows. This was serious business.

"I'll stay right here," she said and picked at the gruffy part of Tay Tay's ear where she'd dripped grape jelly when she was four.

He nodded, leveled the shotgun toward the kitchen, and marched to the back screen door. Clunk Clunk Clunk Clunk.

Annabelle hopped from her bed and got ready for the school bus, hoping it would show up this time. She wasn't worried about Dad. He'd make his way to the back porch, shimmy under the busted 2x4 railing, and peek around the corner with his back pressed tight to the weathered shiplap siding. He'd inspect the gnarly swamp oak that scraped the shingles over his bedroom window when the wind blew. He'd raise the shotgun at it, then spot the green tarp draped over the shovel and grain-laden wheelbarrow. The tarp would flap in the breeze, and he'd draw in a tight breath and pull the trigger. A rush of surprise would wash over him, and he'd wince and grit his teeth when he realized the shotgun wasn't loaded. He'd pull the other trigger, click, then yell something like, 'Charlie in the trees' or 'Charlie in the bushes, boys' as he scrambled into the house.

It was not uncommon for her days to start this way. With Dad either standing in the center of the living room, staring off into space like a zombie, or naked and chasing Charlies in the side yard and all over the pasture. Occasionally, he spent his mornings hunkered down on the pantry floor, re-arranging the jars of canned vegetables. Those were pleasant mornings.

By now he was retreating to his bedroom, scouring the high closet shelf for a box of shotgun shells. He wouldn't find them. She'd moved those to the secret cubby she'd dug out at the corner of the barn three weeks ago. He'd give up, prop the shotgun against the closet corner, and crawl into bed. He slept naked because the air conditioner didn't work anymore.

Dad simply wasn't the same ever since he died and came back to life. Ever since the afternoon she found him collapsed in the attic. He must've been tinkering with the air conditioner because it had been leaking water through the bathroom ceiling. Painted a large, bean-shaped, saturation in the drywall just above the toilet. She came in from fishing and he was there, passed out with his tools scattered all over, the stench of charred hair and electric ozone wafting the air around him. Sensing something wasn't right, she pressed her ear to his nose, and realized he wasn't breathing.

She rolled him over to see his face and check his neck pulse, and he tumbled down the rickety attic stairs and thudded onto his back. He'd flopped down like a real Raggedy Andy with his bottom half lumped sideways over his torso and his arms spread like Jesus. The fall must've jolted life back into him because by the time she climbed down to help, he'd started breathing again. She sat with him and combed her fingers through his wiry red hair. Eventually he woke up, and she guided him to his bed, but he was never the same person after that. Either the electric shock or the fall down the stairs turned him into an oogie head. Probably both and being dead for a while gave him wonky brains. That's why he acted so strangely.

Annabelle tied her white sneakers and hefted her purple JanSport backpack. She gripped the brass doorknob with both hands and gave it a firm tug. The outside air was breezy and thick that morning, the sky overcast, billowy shades of gray. She trekked along the left rut path until she reached the washout spot in the driveway and weaved over to the right one. As she neared, a lumpy brown toad hopped away for the patches of thick Johnson grass that skirted the driveway. She whistled a three-note tune to it as she passed, low-high-low, good-morn-ing.

Theirs was the only mailbox on Crabtree Road. She stood next to it and dropped her backpack to lean against the splintered cedar post base. Across the street stood a tangle of underbrush blanketed in kudzu. A long time ago, a little clapboard farmhouse was there. Now it was a slumped over heap of rubble, slowly being swallowed by nature. Far to her left was the asphalt road, Walters, where the bus would appear and turn onto Crabtree if it was coming today. She didn't know.

They were somewhere in the middle of summer break when Dad had his accident, and it seemed like they'd been out of school a long time. Seemed like school started again around the time the weather got chilly, but some years it stayed hot for a good while in Texas. There was no way for her to tell when it started again. Best to be safe and go out every morning until the bus showed up. School was important to her.

Dad didn't believe in school. He didn't believe in church or doctors either. That's why she didn't call for an ambulance the day he died and came back to life. He didn't believe in phones, radio, television, or even clocks. After she turned five, he kept her home for a year and a half until a black man with glasses and a moustache came from the county and told him he had to let her go to school. Annabelle smiled bright that day and celebrated in the barn so Dad wouldn't see her so happy about something that brought him the grumbles, baked a fat pan of sweet bread with extra honey and shared it with the chickens in the barn.

Annabelle waited for what felt like an hour and peered down the long swath of gravely road to the blacktop of Walters until her eyes went all screwy and she had to blink them to make the road straight again. Then she watched two brown squirrels argue over the climbing rights to a puny hackberry tree. Then she peered down the road again. She imagined the orange-yellow school bus appearing in the distance, lurch around the bend, get bigger as it droned up Crabtree Road, and hiss-squeaked to a stop in the gravel before her. It never came. She sat for a while and tossed pebbles, then picked up her backpack and walked home.

Dad was asleep when she got to the house. The air inside was turning warm and stale, so she left the front door open to let in the breeze. She changed from her first-day-of-school outfit to her everyday clothes, then made her way to the kitchen to make a peanut-butter-and-jelly for breakfast. The peanut butter jar was nearly empty, so she scraped the butter knife along the inside edges to pull up the last little bit. She made one for Dad also and left it at his spot at the kitchen table, blanketed with a paper towel to shield it from flies. She went out the back kitchen door.

Annabelle scanned the pasture for their dairy cow Nell   as she walked across the back yard for the big red barn. She spotted a mottled splotch of creamy brown munching among the tall green buffalo grass at the far corner of the pasture. Dad usually shredded the pasture around this time to have hay stored for Nell to eat through the winter. She worried he wouldn't this year. She turned the spigot handle and watched as tiny tadpoles and minnows scurried in frantic circles and figure-eights in Nell's concrete drinking trough as it filled up.

Next, she took the blue bucket by the handle and carried it into the barn to hunt for eggs. She found the first clutch in its normal spot under the green-and-yellow tractor. From there, she turned for the hay. All that remained from winter was four bales—scattered amber heaps, like tiny sleeping bulls. Two of them were occupied. A red hen sat on one and a brown hen sat on the other, perched pristine like lady guardians of the morning. The brown hen gave a cackle and ran away, flapping and flustered when Annabelle lifted her and nabbed three eggs from her nest. The red hen didn't wait for her to lift her. She perked to attention and fled just as she came near.

Annabelle's eyes widened. The red hen had four eggs in her nest. She usually keeps exact pace with the brown hen. She should only have three. Annabelle reached for the first egg which was speckled purple. She swiped to rub the speckles away with her thumb. They didn't come away, and she'd left a thumb-sized divot in the shell where she pressed. This wasn't a chicken egg at all. It was the size of a ping-pong ball, perfectly round, and leathery like a snake egg. How bizarre.

She thought to hurl it against the tractor grill and watch it splat. She certainly wasn't going to eat it or feed it to her dad. She raised her arm and took aim, then paused. Something moved inside. She imagined a tiny alligator embryo turning squirmy flips. A tingle radiated through her fingertips in a buzzy vibration, like gripping the refrigerator handle in the still of night. There was something special about this egg. Something incredible and strange. She set it on the other three and carried the bucket to the house.

Dad was carrying his fishing pole through the side pasture when she came to the back porch. The fishing rod flopped with his footsteps. A red and white cork jostled around the slender tip of the rod as he tromped through the tall grass. He carried the peanut butter sandwich in his other hand, shrouded nicely in the paper towel.

"Going fishing?" she called to him.

"You got it, sister," he called with a wink.

She smiled, "look out for snakes."

He pretended to spot a snake in the grass, gave an animated hop backward, then charged to stomp it under his bootheel.

Sometimes he acted perfectly normal. This made her feel good—a welling of joy lifted her up the porch steps. Then she looked back and noticed the end of his fishing line was rigged with a number two circle hook strung through a fat brown cigar. Her heart sank a little.

She stepped into the kitchen and set the blue bucket on the counter. She lifted the tap lever and gave each egg a quick rinse and towel-down, saving the purple-spotted one for last. When she came to that one, she inspected it closely. The leathery shell was supple under her fingers, and she felt it would pop and burst something warm and gooey, maybe grape jelly, all over the walls if she squeezed it. She didn't. She carried the bizarre little nugget to her room, turning it over and eyeing it along the way.

She plopped onto her bed, kicked off her shoes, and pushed Tay Tay Bear aside. Then she rolled over and clicked on the metallic purple reading lamp at her nightstand. It shone down to the floor. She twisted the neck to point at her, winced from the blinding light, and peered at the egg. She held it between her thumb and index finger and looked closer, eclipsing the light slowly back and forth. Shadowy globules were along the edges, and the middle was lumpy shades of translucent purple. Again, something moved inside, wriggled against her thumb, and she nearly dropped the egg. Was it ready to hatch?

She moved her blue plastic water cup to the opposite nightstand. She was thirsty most nights, especially since the air conditioner went out. Then she gathered several socks and her raggedy Navasota Rattlers Football shirt and piled them into a nest on her nightstand. She tucked the egg into a divot in the middle and admired how nicely the little sphere matched the size of the nest–if only her socks and the Navasota Rattlers colors were lavender instead of white and blue.

Next, she fiddled with the neck of the reading lamp until the bulb radiated just enough heat on the egg without scalding it. She wriggled her fingers under the light and watched the speckled egg. It shimmered. She looked closer. The purple speckles weren't speckles at all. They were translucent spots in the shell like tiny oval windows. She found the biggest one and squinted at it. What she was seeing as purple speckles was the embryo, the yolk, or maybe the skin of the creature inside. She wasn't certain.

Satisfied her marvelous egg was cozy and well incubated, she pulled Tay Tay Bear to her chest and read to him, Green Eggs and Ham, stopping to glance at the egg with each turn of the page. Just as Sam I Am had The Grump nearly convinced he would let down his defenses and try the green eggs and ham, while drifting on the ocean with a goat, a fox, a mouse, and several other whimsical characters looking on, the kitchen door slammed, and Dad's voice boomed to her down the hallway.

"You're never gonna get my cabbages. You dirty sonofabitch!"

A flurry of panic jolted her to her feet. She rushed to the kitchen to find the fishing pole lying on the floor, soggy cigar splatted limp, like a dog turd, on the cream ceramic tile next to the trash can. There was Dad, holding something lumpy and heavy. He was gripping it with the same heft he would use on a rumbling chainsaw, and he slammed it to the kitchen table with the concrete thud of a cinder block.

It was swamp green, with spiked ridges along the back. It hissed, and she realized what it was - a lunker of a snapping turtle, the size of a basketball, and thoroughly pissed off. Dad's left arm was ripped open. Blood trickled from his wrist to the elbow and his hand was smeared slick crimson. He had to have been bitten at least twice by the prehistoric creature. And still he didn't care; he was determined to get something valuable from the turtle, something it took from him. Cabbages? But they didn't grow cabbages. They didn't even have a garden this year.

"Let it go, Daddy," she cried.

Dad leaned forward and tilted his head to be level with the turtle. The snapper had retreated into his shell, beak open and ready to strike. It twitched, and its laser focus on Dad's face said, "Come any closer and I'll rip another gash in your looney ass."

A hiss, followed by a thunky clomp. That noise was the turtle striking so fast his head was only a blur at Dad's nose and back, barely missing. She remembered Mrs. Sullivan at school, telling the class about how a snapper could clamp a tree limb in half and easily do the same to a full-grown man's fingers. Dad winced and pulled his face back. Then he raised his fingers and said, "It's in there sooomewhere."

"Noooo, Daddy!" She grabbed his elbow.

The shrill in her voice frightened her and startled Dad to his senses. Her face was slick with tears.

"Daddy, stop!"

He didn't. He swiped two fingers at the snapper's beak. It hissed and twitched. Then she remembered something. She took a schoolmarm pose, left hand on hip, right index finger pointed stiff and stern at Dad's face.

"Silas Theodore Riley," she shouted.

Dad pulled away from the snapping turtle and looked at her, eyebrows raised. Then his face took the dopey expression of a ten-year-old boy caught with his hand in the cookie jar. He stood straight, at attention, and his arms went behind his back.

"Silas, you leave that poor critter alone! Leave it right there, and you get your filthy bee-hind to the bathroom and wash up. Now!" She stamped her foot.

He clambered for the bathroom and slammed the door.

She'd learned this trick, pretending to be his mom or a teacher, she wasn't sure which one he saw, one evening when she was going through his wallet in search of grocery money. This was before she learned he didn't carry cash because the VA deposited money into the bank card. She came to his driver's license and realized she never actually knew his middle name. She'd read it aloud, "Silas Theodore Riley."

He sat up in his recliner with a childish, "Yes ma'am?"

His smirk told her she was addressing a little boy, so she played along. "Silas, you show me where the money is so I can take my backpack to town and get us some noodles and flour."

He hunkered down on the living room floor next to her, crisscross applesauce, and fiddled with the wallet until he produced the red Wells Fargo Visa card. Then he held it up in triumph, and she told him he was a good boy.

She hadn't used this trick before, but she kept it tucked in a corner nook in her memories for an emergency, and this was certainly one.

She went outside, rounded the corner, and spotted the handles of the wheelbarrow, sticking out from the green tarp. A shovel leaned against the wheelbarrow. She pulled the tarp away and dumped the grain on the ground. She was doubtful Dad was keeping a heap of grain in the wheelbarrow for something specific. He probably simply forgot it there, and Nell and the chickens would surely find it, so dumping it wouldn't be a waste.

She tossed the shovel into the wheelbarrow and hefted it to the back porch. She lumbered the wheelbarrow around and tried pulling it backward, but quickly realized she was too small to get the legs over the steps. She'd have to bring the turtle outside.

When she came in, Dad was singing 'The Itsy Bitsy Spider' in the bathtub. He was likely bleeding to death, but she was too exasperated to check. The snapping turtle was locked into retreat mode—a swampy lump of angry spikes on the kitchen table. Its jagged tail was sticking out, and the mouth opened and hissed when she neared it.

"Don't worry, buddy. I'm going to take you home. Sorry about my dad. He's not feeling well," she said and patted the turtle's shell.

She lifted the turtle from the table with all her strength, holding it close to her belly like a sack of potatoes. It wasn't quite as heavy as she imagined, and once she got the tail rested against her bellybutton, the going got easier. The claws scraped at her arms and the beak reached up to snap at her neck, but she was extra mindful to hold that end far out of skin's reach.

She took careful steps, slow and steady, to the screen door and shouldered it open. The turtle snapped for the door handle and nearly got it. Once outside, on the porch, she bent her knees to slide the turtle down the front lip of the wheelbarrow but ended up thumping it in with a heavy thud.

"Sorry," she said and swiped her hands clean.

The turtle landed upside down and immediately reached out its long neck and used its nose as a pivot to flip itself over. The snapper was much more athletic than pond turtles, full of vigor like she imagined a dinosaur would be.

Again, she hefted the wheelbarrow handles and made her way through the tall pasture. Nell was still munching at the buffalo grass at the far corner. Now she was under a puny hackberry tree. As she trudged through the thick grass, fat grasshoppers leaped from the path, skittered in the air, and fluttered down to land somewhere safe. The snapping turtle stayed perfectly still, tucked in its home, with only the tip of the tail poking out. She fixed her gaze on the creek line in the distance and grimaced.

They came to the gulley that marked the halfway point. She was sweating and her shoulders and forearms ached. She let the handles down and picked a splinter from her reddened palm. She looked back and expected to see Dad, maybe dangling from the barn roof like a monkey, maybe running after them with the green tarp draped around his neck like a cape, but he wasn't there. Hopefully he didn't manage to drown himself in the bathtub somehow.

She breathed deep, gripped the wheelbarrow handles again, and lifted. They came up easier with her frustration. She imagined herself a raging bull, planted the balls of her feet and charged. The wheelbarrow rumbled. The turtle bounced. She didn't care. She lifted her knees and trotted, then sprinted. A maddening grin inched across her face. They picked up speed and traveling was easy; the wheelbarrow bounced along. She no longer felt the smacks from the stiff grasses at her shins.

"Hang on," she called to the snapping turtle, who was now being thoroughly jostled with a hardy 'thunk-thunk' from one side of the metal tub to the other.

'Wham.' The iron nose of the wheelbarrow slammed into a log, hidden under the tall grass. The hind end of the barrow flipped forward, jamming the handle into her chin. Her eyes squeezed shut, and she saw white, then red. Her arms flailed, elbows banged the aluminum wheelbarrow legs, and she was on the ground.

When she came to, she realized her hand was planted in an ant mound. Her knuckle stung, then the other fingers. In a flash, her whole hand was on fire. She smacked at the fuming pesker at her knuckle and saw her arm was speckled black, up to the elbow—tiny black wrigglers, twitching to pinch skin and inject venom. She scrambled to her feet, peeled off her shirt, and swiped them away. The stings kept coming well after all the ants were gone. Her arm swelled red and pulsed. She drew a deep breath and held it tight, then brought her knuckle to her mouth, tongued it, and blew on it.

She stepped onto the log and checked on the snapping turtle. It was flung over, now lumbering away toward the creek line. The nose of the wheelbarrow was bent but not digging into the wheel; it'd be okay. The turtle would be okay too. He'd find his way to the creek. Animals were clever.

She sat on the log and swiped dirt from her hands then spread her shirt and flapped it in the air. She looked at their house, far away in the distance and wanted to cry but didn't. She smiled and looked at the sky.

She stopped at the side of the house on her way in and snapped a sprig of aloe from the potted plant sitting on the white propane tank. She slit the leaf longways with her thumbnail and peeled the flaps open. She slathered the sticky juices all over her hand and arm, wrapping it around her knuckle twice. She closed her eyes and waved her hand through the air to feel the breeze. Much better. Still, her chin ached, and she was pretty sure there was a chipped tooth at the back of her mouth, but there was nothing she could do about that.

The bathroom was warm and dank, and three bloodied towels littered the floor. The tub was drained with a small pool of red-tinged water leftover at the bottom. She went to Dad's bedroom. He was dozing on his side with the window fan blowing on him full blast.

She sat on his bed and pulled his arm out from under the blanket. His wrist was mangled. A gash was torn from just below the boney knob under the wrist. She judged it was the length of a pen cap and as deep as her pinky finger was wide. The skin flaps wobbled when she moved his hand and a piece of flesh pulsed red.

She thought of all the gross swamp stuff living around the snapping turtle's mouth. It might get infected, and he'd have to go to the doctor. She almost wanted that, but he'd likely refuse.

She went outside and snapped another sprig of aloe, then rummaged through the kitchen drawer until she came to the super glue squirter. The tube was nearly empty, and the cap was caked shut with glue, so she worked it free with the kitchen shears and cut a new opening below the tip. There was no Neosporin or alcohol in the medicine cabinet, hardly anything: fingernail clippers, tweezers, a bar of soap, and dental floss. Dad didn't believe in pills or ointments.

Dad woke up when she started fiddling with his arm. He moved to sit up, but she put her hand on his forehead and coaxed him to lay back. He winced when she wiped the wound clean with the aloe sprig. She pinched the wound closed with her fingers and dripped super glue over the flaps. Then she counted to twenty and did it twice more. Finally, she held her breath and let go. Blood trickled from the corners, but the seam stayed together. She pressed the skin around it, and still, it held together.

She slathered aloe over the homemade stitching and tied around his wrist a ripped strand of cotton from one of his old boot socks. He thumbed a strand of hair from her face and tucked it behind her ear.

"You're a good girl," he said and smiled.

***

That evening they played Castles and Kings. Dad hunkered down on the hardwood floor in the living room and stacked a handful of their blue-backed Bicycle playing cards into a little castle. Annabelle did the same at her spot in the opposite corner of the living room, by the fireplace. Dad was an excellent builder. He concentrated—tongue out, left eye squinting——until the cards lined up perfectly. His castle had three levels with a drawbridge entrance in the middle. Hers had two levels, uneven and sloped wonky at the ends.

Then they took turns flinging marbles at each other's castle. He plucked his. She was allowed to toss hers because her plucks fizzled out before reaching his castle. Still, she managed to win somehow, as always, and when his final barricade tumbled, he lowered his face to the floor in defeat. Then he wrapped his arms around his head and was snoozing like a toddler thirty seconds later. She clicked the window fan to medium, flipped the light switch off, and went to her room.

She pulled Tay Tay Bear to her chest and hugged him as they read Little House on the Prairie, a book she treasured since it was her mom's. The inside of the cover page had: Elizabeth Sewell X Mas 1977, written in blue cursive lettering. She traced her finger over the letters before opening to the page bookmarked with the pink ribbon she'd cut from her tattered hair tie.

After five pages, her eyelids became droopy and her grip on Tay Tay relaxed. She rolled over and clicked off the nightstand light out of habit. Then her eyes widened. The egg was glowing. Her room was bathed in purple with iridescent stars sprinkled on the ceiling and walls like a luminous lavender night sky. She took the egg with her fingers and held it in the air. It was like a laser ball. Purple beams shone in every direction, and when she moved it, the wall-stars shimmered and danced. It reminded her of the glow necklaces and bracelets other kids wore at the county fair, but much, much more brilliant.

She tucked the egg in the nest, clicked the light back on, rolled over, and shrouded herself and Tay Tay Bear under the blanket to sleep in violet shade with a smile curled onto her lips.

***

The next morning, she expected her afternoon ant bites to be bubbled into blisters. She was actually looking forward to the blisters, her reward for suffering through the agony of fire ant bites. She enjoyed the satisfying sensation of pinching them until they popped. She ran a finger along the skin of her right hand, where the bites were supposed to be. Nothing. She double checked the knuckle of her middle finger. That one was the worst. Again. Nothing. The ant bites were gone. How could they be gone? If not yet blistered, they should at least be itchy red welts by now.

She glanced at the egg and picked it up with her right hand, just as she'd done the night before. The egg pulsed a rhythmic hum, and energy skittered through to her fingertips. A thought occurred to her. She tossed the blankets aside, climbed out of bed, and carried the egg into the living room. There, she found dad, still hunkered down on the hardwood floor, now tucked into the fetal position. The cotton wrap had come untied, ribboned among the marbles and playing cards before him. He must've tugged it away in his sleep.

The turtle bite festered, deep red. Her eyes widened. Her superglue stitching had busted open. The aloe she had slathered over it was caked dry and overtaken by lumpy yellow pus. She sat next to him and pulled his arm to her lap. It was coursing with fever. So was his face, and his hair was drenched in sweat. He grunted but didn't lift his head or wake up.

She took the egg into the palm of her hand and rolled it over the wound. She made circles around it, then rolled it through the cut and back again like dumpling dough through flour. Dad winced, pulled his arm away, and tucked it under his chest. She thought some of the yellow pus dried up and wilted into flecks, but she wasn't sure. His hand moved away too fast.

She returned the egg to its nest on her bedside table. It moved when she put it down. Something from inside, she imagined a foot, pushed against the leathery shell to make an eraser-sized bump appear on the surface. The bump glided from the bottom of the shell to the top, then disappeared. She smiled.

She dressed herself for school, tied her white sneakers, and hefted her purple JanSport backpack. The outside air was cooler than yesterday, still and dry. Fall was coming. Hopefully school would start soon. Maybe the bus would come today, and she'd go to a place that was…normal…predictable…safe. –Where she had control over her own successes. W–here there were successes: friends, teachers, volleyball, math quizzes, Tutankhamun, George Washington, chilly bus rides, storytelling monster puppets, hamburgers, fruit cocktails, and chocolate milk.

She trekked along the left rut path, and when she reached the washout spot in the driveway, a little toad sat on top of a big toad at the edge of the puddle. She whistled a three-note tune to them as she passed, low-high-low, good-morn-ing. She hopped the puddle.

At the road, a brown fox snuck into the kudzu underbrush across the street. She dropped her backpack to lean against the splintered cedar mailbox post. The fox spotted her and crouched with his left paw frozen mid-step. They locked gazes for what she thought was a very long time——long enough for the vegetation around the fox to go blurry in her vision.

A rumble came to her from the end of Crabtree Road. Then it hiss-squeaked to a stop. Her heart leapt in her chest, and she reached for her backpack. But when she looked up, it was only a big blue garbage truck. It lumbered past her, making more noise than she thought was needed for a truck traveling so slowly. The driver smiled at her from under his square green cap and waved. She waved to him but didn't smile.

She looked for the fox, but it had slinked away, probably to his den, or to hunt crawfish and perch at the creek behind the rotted clapboard house across the road. She wouldn't see him again that day.

She waited at the end of the driveway even after she knew the school bus wasn't coming. Maybe tomorrow. She thought about something and enjoyed the brisk air and watched the kudzu thicket for the fox even though she didn't expect him to come back. After a long while, she lifted her backpack and walked home.

Dad was pacing on the front porch with a butcher knife in his left hand. He mumbled something to himself and pointed the knife at the front door, then slashed it through the air. A cringe gripped her. What was it now?

She stopped at the lavender rhododendrons a few feet in front of the first porch step, well shy of slashing reach. Dad's mad eye locked onto her, and his eyebrows went up.

"There you are," he said and hopped down the steps, skipping two and nearly tripping over his feet at the bottom.

She glanced at the knife and moved to turn and run, but he went to his knees before her and reached his arms out for a hug. At the worry and confusion in his eyes, she fell into him. Her heart thudded in her chest.

"I thought they took you," he said with a tinge of whimper in his voice and gripped her shoulders.

"Who?" she asked and looked at the front door.

"Somebody's been in the house, Annie," he said. His eyes widened when he loosened the grip of his left hand and showed her the evidence.

She saw three marbles and two crumpled playing cards—the two of diamonds and queen of hearts. Behind the hand, his face was slick and pale.

Her shoulders dropped, and she drew a deep breath.

Then he waved the knife toward the front door, "All over the place in there! Thank God, you're okay. I didn't find anything missing. Can't figure out what they took from us. But all that matters is nobody got hurt, and you're okay. You're okay, right? Did they try to touch you?"

She scrambled through her head to find the right words. Trying to convince him of something he would never remember was useless.

"I'm okay, Daddy. Nobody tried to get me. I need to tell you something," she said.

He nodded.

"I took the marbles and cards out last night after you fell asleep and forgot to put them up," she said, "Then this morning, I went to catch the school bus, but it never came."

He glanced toward the road and tilted his head with a spiteful grimace. "They probably figured out all the lies and burned that place down, I figure." He stood and guided her by the small of her back up the porch steps. "Well, it's a good thing you fessed up. I was worried real bad. Go on and pick up the mess as best you can." he said.

"Yes, sir," she said, took the marbles and cards from his hand, and flattened the cards against the porch rail to straighten them.

He went inside, poured his hind end into his recliner, and looked at the ceiling, then rested his eyes while she picked up the marbles and playing cards and dropped them into the rust-speckled Folgers can. She slid the can onto the fireplace mantle next to Dad's recliner.

He breathed deep. She rolled his arm over and found the wound was healed. Incredible! A turtle bite like that should take weeks to go away, but here it was, perfectly healed. All that was left was a bumpy scar, like a pink earthworm buried under his skin, no yellow pus, no festering skin flaps. She felt his head. No fever. The fever in his arm was gone too, and the swelling down. He was healed. The mysterious egg had some kind of special powers. She smiled and went to her room.

She loosened the straps of her backpack with a sigh and let it fall to the floor. Then she kicked off her shoes. A rush of energy skittered up her spine. Goosebumps bristled her arm hairs, and her vision narrowed.

The egg had hatched. The nest was there, with the purple lamp shining down on it, just as she'd left them, but the leathery eggshell was slit from bottom to top, and mucus goo drizzled out. But the creature was gone. She scanned the hardwood floor as she stepped ginger-footed to the nightstand, socks sliding. It could be anywhere.

She lifted the shell and examined it—the purple speckles were gone now. It was like a floppy ping pong ball bisected with a surgeon's knife. She placed the shell on the nightstand and pulled apart the makeshift nest, piece-by-piece, but found nothing. Some of the socks were snotty and a dollop of egg white licked her pinky finger. She sniffed it. Chemical-ey? With a hint of strawberry pudding?

She nudged the lamp aside, moved her hairbrush, and checked under her stack of books–as if a tiny creature could be hiding under books. She pulled open the nightstand drawer: hair berets, rubber bands, two shiny rocks, a peppermint candy cane, and the pink Bible Grandma Rodgers gave her with the cartoon lamb smiling at her from the cover. She went to her knees and looked under her bed: a wad of paper towels, heavy feather blanket, sleeping bag, Scrabble, Candy Land, Jenga, and her missing cherry sweater were all she could make out from that side. She'd have to find the flashlight to see the rest.

Then she checked her bed. Tay Tay Bear looked at her from his spot at her pillow. She lifted him so they were nose to nose and asked, "You haven't seen a new little fella around here, have you?" as she carried him to the closet and set him on the floor. Then she took the pillows. Nothing was under them except the silk edges of her green comforter. She surveyed the blanket and imagined finding a little purple frog, hatchling chick, or maybe even a tiny chicken-frog. All she saw was a rumpled hunter-green blanket with tattered stitching in two places, and a pink sock. She thought she felt the slightest hint of moisture as she balled up the blanket and tossed it onto the pillows and Tay Tay, but that could've been leftover sweat from last night. Her room was hot ever since the air conditioning went out, and she didn't have a fan.

She came back to the bed and sat next to the nightstand opposite the side she slept, watching Tay Tay peek at her from behind the pillows in her closet. She brought the blue plastic cup to her mouth, then paused to try to remember when she last filled it with fresh water. She glanced inside. A glowing purple creature swam in frantic circles at the bottom.

She caught her breath and put the cup down. Then she waited for a three count and peeked over the edge. Five tentacles, octopus arms, reached out like star-points from the center. They were a bit too long for the bottom of the cup and curled at the ends. Beedy black eyes peered at her from just above a green-striped parrot's beak. The back of the head was lined with ripples and bumps. Something glowed from inside the head, and the ripples fluttered. They fluttered from top to bottom, then bottom to top, left to right, right to left, then faster than a heartbeat. Was it trying to talk to her?

"Hi," she said and wiggled her index finger at it.

It watched her, and the feeling she got from its blank expression was doleful with a hint of confusion, like a frightened baby animal. The ripples fluttered from bottom to top, slowly, then faster and faster. She tried to think of what it could be trying to say and realized it was under stress. Something moved at the neck. Gills. They fluttered also, but not as fast as the glowing head-ripples, and they gasped for breath every other second. It was suffocating. It needed water. The cup was barely filled enough to cover the octopus arms, and the gills were struggling to breathe.

She went to the kitchen and brought back a glass mason jar filled with fresh tap water. Dad was gone from his recliner when she crossed the hallway entrance. She glanced around but was too busy to search for him. She thought she heard something outside, a thump against a wall maybe, or an ax thwacking firewood, but shrugged it off.

She hustled the mason jar to her bed, set it on the nightstand, and poured the plastic cup into it. The water came out, but not the creature. She looked inside, and found it glued to the bottom, The frills fluttered and now the eyes glowed purple also. It was terrified to come out.

She turned the cup upside down and held it over the rim of the mason jar. She thought to tap the bottom of the cup but worried that might scare it even more.

After a while, just when her arm muscles were burning enough to want to put the cup down and give up, it plopped out. The tiny creature dangled from the lip of the cup and reached a tentacle into the mason jar. The tentacle swirled around to test the water, then it slinked in.

The creature swirled to the bottom of the mason jar, made two laps, and investigated the glass with its tentacles. It had knowing eyes, and they looked at her face when she peered in. The head ripples fluttered, and the gills breathed like she hoped was normal, no more gasping. It seemed more comfortable.

She set the jar on the nightstand, where the nest was.

"Hi," she said and wiggled her index finger at the creature.

There came a pause, then it lifted a tentacle, and her fingertip met it on the glass surface. Warm energy buzzed into her finger through the glass. She smiled and somehow knew it was smiling too. The ripples fluttered at a peaceful tempo.

"This is my room. We live in Texas; that's Grimes County USA. You're not from around here, are you?" she asked with a shake of her head.

The creature didn't move.

"Well, I'm Annabelle Elizabeth Riley, and this is Tay Tay Bear," she said and lifted Tay Tay for the introduction. The creature moved to see him. "He likes grape jelly and storybooks." She tossed Tay Tay aside, "Don't worry. He's not a real bear. You're real though. Aren't you? I am, too."

She moved her fingertip to make circles on the surface of the glass. The creature lifted a tentacle and did the same.

"I think I'll call you Molly Marbles because your egg was like a magic marble. Are you hungry?" she asked and thought for a moment. Then she got an idea, lifted a finger as if to say, 'just one sec', and hopped from the bed and left the room.

After some time, she came back with a collection of goodies in the overturned flap of her untucked T-shirt. She lifted the flap and spread the contents on the bedside table, careful not to spill: a handful of Honey Nut Cheerios, two rhododendron flower petals, a nugget of Dad's spicy beef jerky, the end of a mini peppermint candy cane she found in the silverware drawer, four sprigs of fescue grass, an oak leaf, an angry earthworm, and chicken scratch grain; cracked corn, millet, wheat, milo, and sunflower seed. The earthworm flitted for a few moments, then gave up and searched along the tabletop for something soft to burrow into.

She dropped two Cheerios into the water and studied the creature's reaction. Its frills flickered twice, and it climbed up the side of the jar to be closer. She admired how the suckers made perfect squishy circles on the surface of the glass. Were octopus suckers like that— lively and clever like human fingers. She wanted to feel it on her arm–, if it would hold on and wrap around.

Maybe she'd try to fling it off with a flick of her wrist to test how strong the suckers were. Maybe another time.

Suspended at the middle of the jar, Molly reached a timid tentacle toward a cheerio and tapped it. The cheerio jiggled. The tentacle pulled away and came back to twine itself through the hole and wrap around. Was it tasting with its hands?

The green beak moved, and a tiny bubble came out, then all at once, it released the cheerio and slinked to the bottom. She peered over the edge. Two cheerios bobbed on the surface. She picked them out and replaced them with a kernel of corn and sunflower. They floated too.

The response she got from the corn and sunflower kernels was the same. Molly climbed up to investigate, then lost interest and retreated after a few light touches. It crunched the rhododendron petals and brought one of them toward her eyes to see closer, but soon let it go to drift a couple inches below the surface of the water. She used the end of her hairbrush to fish them out.

Next in line was the peppermint candy. She reached for it, but her attention was diverted to the earthworm wriggling dangerously close to the edge of the nightstand. She picked it up. It tried to wrap itself around her fingers but gave up and dangled in the shape of a hook.

She dropped the earthworm in, and specks of black soil flecked from its skin to drift on the surface. The worm wriggled, free and clean, and glided toward the bottom. Its waggy movement was mesmerizing to her.

Just as fast as the snapping turtle snapping for Dad's nose, Molly shot two tentacles up and snatched the worm. It jerked it down and curled into a knot of writhing muscle at the bottom of the jar.

The knot pulsed, and the green beak and eyes disappeared, along with the worm, somewhere inside the tangle of tentacles. She drew a quick breath and watched in amazement. Soon, Molly relaxed, and her head-ripples flashed brilliant shades of green. She smiled and clapped her hands, just as she did when the teacher finished reading a good storybook in class.

Flecks of earthworm flesh scattered from Molly's spot at the bottom. It used its tentacles, picked them from the water, and brought them to its beak, one-by-one, with a glaze of satisfaction over its face.

"So, you're a bug eater?" she asked. "Well, that's okay. We've got plenty of bugs around here for you. We live on a farm."

The clunk of Dad's boots came to her from the hallway. She wiped the scattered mess of test-foods into the nightstand drawer and rushed Molly's jar to the closet. She tucked it into the back corner, behind Tay Tay Bear and the pillows and whispered, "Don't worry. I'll be back. I just don't want my dad to see you yet."

Bare-chested, Dad appeared in her doorway, wearing a dopey grin. His hands and wrists were stained green for some bizarre reason. They looked as though they'd been smeared in paint, then rinsed, poorly. Green handprints decorated his chest, one just above each nipple; right over left, left over right. His cheeks sported double green finger stripes to match, and the tip of his nose was smeared green also, but that wasn't war paint. That was from him swiping at an itch carelessly. He stood in silence, his brains having an extra wonky moment.

"What are you up to?" she asked after what seemed like a very long time of him glaring at the window curtains and ceiling, then at her.

His lower lip jutted, and he shook his head as if to say 'nuthin'.

She pointed to his chest, then to her cheeks. "Are you a Comanche warrior?" she asked with a tilt of her head.

A clever grin sidled across his face, and his eyes twinkled.

"It looks good, Daddy," she said with an assuring nod.

She took his hand and guided him to the kitchen. He followed, and his untied boots clunked up the hallway once more. She sat him at the kitchen table and tied his boots for him. He leaned back with the relaxed bearing of a man about to receive an old timey shave.

"I want you to teach me something. Can you teach me something?" she asked and glanced to him.

His gaze met hers.

"You're the best fisherman around these parts, and you already taught me how to fish. But that's with a pole and bobber, for perch mostly. I want to learn how to set a trot line. I think I'm big enough to go after monster catfish like you."

She finished tying his boot and sat in the chair next to him, dangling an elbow over the armrest.

"That'd be good," he said and nodded.

"And here's the thing," she said and leaned into his dim-witted gaze, "I want to use worms. Big worms. Not those little stringy fellas we sometimes get in the puddles when it rains. I'm talkin' about bigguns." She held her index fingers six inches apart to demonstrate. "You think we can find some worms that big?" she asked, "That's whopper sized."

"Whopper wigglers," he said and giggled.

"That's right. Wiggler whopper whopper wigglers."

"Wiggler whopper whopper wiggler," he repeated, then paused and lost himself staring through the window for twelve seconds.

She looked through the window. All she saw was the bright Texas horizon of cornfields and oak trees.

"Let me show you," he said, stood, and marched through the kitchen doorway.

The screen door slammed into her nose when she came to the porch to follow. She fumbled with it and called, "We'll need a bucket."

His response was to continue his march across the back yard without looking back, while pointing both index fingers, and fire fake pistols into the blue, clear sky.

She heaved an exasperated sigh and grabbed the blue chicken egg bucket from the porch, then followed him.

Nell, the jersey cow, was sipping from her concrete water trough when Annabelle made the porch landing. She waved to her then she saw their red barn was now splotched all over with green man handprints, in toddler fashion; smeared wonky in places and perfect in others, all at Dad height. The gallon paint bucket, John Deere Green, was dumped sideways at the corner of the barn and paint oozed onto the gravel walkway.

He continued his march into the pasture. She trotted after.

A red hen scurried from the barn when she neared, and she giggled. The hen was wearing a green handprint saddle.

She caught up to him as he was traveling through the pasture to the cadence of a chant, "Wiggler. Whopper. Whopper. Wiggler."

She swung the blue bucket along with the beat and took his hand, and they marched together. She looked at the sky and somewhere deep inside, she thought she'd like for her dad to be an oogie head forever.

He took her to the rotted log in the middle of the pasture. The same rotted log she'd crashed the wheelbarrow into the day before.

"Look out. There's fire ants around here somewhere," she said and searched the ground, but the buffalo grass was too thick for her to find the mound.

He went to the end of the log and worked his burly fingers under the edge. He groaned and his face went red, then the massive oak cracked and moved. Now he was standing with the rotted root ball at his chest. He grunted again and heaved it aside. Then he took a champion's pose and pounded his chest like a gorilla.

"Ha!" she blurted, then grinned and applauded.

He pointed at the ground and said, "Whopper… Wiggler," punctuating each word with a nod of his head.

The newly exposed soil was rich, black, and swarming with life. June bugs, grubs, termites, ants, worms, and crickets all scurried for cover from the broad daylight.

She picked a couple of white grubs from their burrows and tossed them into the bucket. Surely Molly would appreciate them just as much as earthworms. Next, she spotted the pointy tail of a worm, dancing in the sunlight. She pinched for it, but it slinked into the soil. Dad grabbed a handful of dirt all around, like a monster crane uprooting a tree, and when his hand came up, half the earthworm was exposed and flopping. She pulled it. The worm made itself fat but eventually came free. It was the size of an ink pen.

Dad pointed, winked, and said, "Whopper?" with raised eyebrows.

"Whopper." She nodded.

She dropped it in the bucket. Another smaller worm was loosened from Dad's crane-grab. It writhed and skittered on the surface. Dad plucked it up with a pinch of his fingers and dropped it in.

She found two more at the edge of the newly exposed soil. She drizzled loose dirt over their collection in the bucket until she was satisfied the critters had enough to burrow into, then she sat in the cool grass and watched Dad search on hands and knees for more. His palms were filthy, stained green and black, and the handprints on his chest smeared from sweat. He searched with the innocent countenance of an adventurous boy. His gaze darted from burrow to dirt clod to rotted bits of tree bark. He worked his finger into an interesting spot in the soil, then pretended to slurp a worm from the hole. When he grinned at her, his cheeks glistened. The sun shone down on her face, and she was happy, and he was happy, too.

She counted seven total by the time they were done. Three whopper wigglers, three normal wigglers, and one baby. With those, four June bugs, and the two grubs, they should be able to keep Molly fed for at least a couple of days.

Dad held her hand as they walked home through the tall buffalo grass pasture. His hand was strong and knotty, like a tree limb, but also tender and kind. He yawned up to the sky and his eyes went sleepy. Still, he smiled at her, and she wondered what, if anything, he was thinking.

***

That evening, Annabelle noticed Molly had grown bigger already. She brought her jar to the nightstand and clicked on the light. The water had become murky with a purple shimmer, like a galaxy jar Mrs. Sullivan showed them in class last year. Though Molly's jar wasn't quite as cloudy with cosmic glitter swirls as Mrs. Sullivan's, it would be soon if Annabelle didn't change the water.

She could still see Molly clearly, who'd surely grown. Her beak and head were bigger, and the tentacles curled farther up, closer to her body, to fit at the bottom of the jar. The eyes had grown wider also, and for a moment, Annabelle caught the slightest hint of whites around the edges, like human eyes.

Annabelle closed her bedroom door. She didn't have to worry about Dad. He was in the recliner in the living room, snoozing hard from his big afternoon of painting, whopper wiggler hunting, and searching the pasture for his lost friends, Lieutenant Broadnax and Captain Trevor. They were never found.

Molly's ripples flashed green and purple when she saw Annabelle lift the first earthworm from the blue bucket. It was the pen sized whopper. She didn't get a chance to drop it in. Three of Molly's tentacles met the worm's tail at the rim of the jar and snatched it down.

"My goodness," Annabelle exclaimed.

The purple muscle ball worked at the bottom of the jar, and Annabelle caught glimpses of brown worm segments among the hungry purple tentacles, but only in brief snatches. It was gone within seven seconds, and Molly collected the drifting scraps as her gills gasped for breath.

"You're a hungry little lady, aren't you?"

Annabelle scraped the dirt around at the bottom of the bucket. She pulled up a grub.

"How about one more?" she asked, "I don't know if you'll like these. They're kind of like worms, but they're white with little brown heads and arms. Fish like 'em plenty."

She brought the grub to the rim of the jar. The grub uncurled, and the tiny arms worked at something invisible in the air before it. Two eager tentacles searched the shiny skin of the grub. A tentacle tip brushed the pad of her finger. She winced and smiled. Molly pulled the plump morsel down and darted for the bottom of the jar. The grub was gone in an instant.

Annabelle situated the blue bucket and one of her favorite books, The Very Hungry Caterpillar, to stand in front of the jar and shield it from view of the doorway. Molly could sleep on the nightstand next to her that night. Dad seldom stepped closer than the doorway when he came in, and even if he did, she could easily distract him from looking on the nightstand. The book would be a good enough barrier for now. She clicked off the light.

She snuggled Tay Tay, and together, they watched Molly's magical purple glow shimmer against the walls and ceiling. Her frills glistened blue and thrummed in rhythmic pulses at the bottom of the jar.

Annabelle watched Molly until her eyelids became heavy, and she could no longer wrestle them open. She rolled over and slept comfy in the purple-tinged twilight. At some point, deep in the still and hollow part of the night, she thought she remembered rolling over and glimpsing one of Molly's tentacles wagging over the edge of the jar and pointing for the blue bucket.

***

Annabelle woke up to a surprise and quickly realized she had seen Molly pointing over the edge of the jar. The nightstand was splattered with dirt-water. The book was tumbled to the floor and the blue bucket streaked with mud. She looked inside the bucket. All she saw was a thin layer of slop. She twined a finger through the mud. No worms. No grubs. The June bugs were gone too. Molly must've climbed out in the middle of the night and gobbled up her entire cache of feed worms.

The water level of Molly's jar was much lower, and the inside of the jar was a cosmic purple swirl, dotted with circle-shaped suckers and blots of Molly's skin pressed against the glass in places. She was much bigger now, and the jar barely contained her. The dome of her head jutted up from the surface like a skin-slick island rising from the ocean. Molly squirmed inside the jar and flashed frantic pulses of orange and red signals.

"Well, then," Annabelle exclaimed.

She inched her bedroom door open and peeked out. Dad's recliner was empty, and he was nowhere in sight. She brought Molly's jar and the blue bucket to the kitchen. She filled the bucket with fresh water, a little more than halfway. Then she turned Molly's jar over. Molly's suckers loosened, and she slinked out. Annabelle set the jar on the kitchen counter and peered into the bucket. Molly swirled around at the bottom, inspecting the strange new habitat. Her frills twinkled tones of blue and lavender, to the tempo of a creative and exploring tune. The bucket was bigger, but still, at this pace, Molly would outgrow it in a day or two. She couldn't keep Molly in the blue bucket, not even for a day. Dad would come looking for it because he used it to carry feed grain to Nell every evening.

At the thought of Nell, an idea came to her. She peered through the kitchen window. There was Nell sipping from her concrete water trough. The trough looked to be the perfect size for Molly to stay in. That would work for now. The bus should be coming soon, and she didn't have time to take Molly all the way to the creek.

She carried Molly's bucket to the back yard and glanced around for Dad. Again, he was nowhere in sight. Nell looked up and lulled a 'good morning' moo to them.

Annabelle waved to her and said, "Hey there, girlie. We're going to let a friend of ours stay in your water trough for a couple of days. Just until we find a bigger place."

Nell reached around and her fat purple tongue lapped at an itchy spot on her shoulder.

Annabelle turned the spigot handle to fill the concrete tank. Dad stepped around the corner of the barn. She tucked the bucket to her chest and shielded the top with her arm. But he wasn't interested in the bucket. He winked at her as he strolled by with a dead snake dangling from the business end of a pitchfork. The snake was fat and black, with a drizzle of blood leaking from the head.

He propped the pitchfork against the weathered porch railing and went inside. Then she turned off the spigot and poured Molly into the concrete water trough. Molly darted for the end of the trough, then worked her tentacles along the algae-coated sides. Again, her frills glowed blue and lavender.

"This'll have to do until tomorrow. I'll try to find you some more worms to eat. Or maybe fish. Do you like fish?"

Next, she took the blue bucket to the barn and collected eggs. Both hens had three. She brought them in through the back screen door and nearly dropped the bucket when she saw Dad drinking the last remaining swill water from Molly's jar. Purple shimmer swirled at the rim, then disappeared down his gullet.

He swallowed heartily and set the jar on the counter. Then his face puckered with confusion, and he grimaced at her.

"Was that beet juice?" he asked.

She set the bucket of eggs on the counter, next to the jar and studied him. "Ummm. I don't think so," she said with a shake of her head.

He doubled over, like he was going to retch into the kitchen sink.

"Dad?" she asked, "Are you okay?"

He caught himself and looked around as though he was seeing the world for the first time. The bewildered grimace relaxed into a glaze of understanding. Then he blinked three times, and his shoulders straightened. In those few moments, something magical had taken hold of him.

"Dad?" she asked.

He glanced through the kitchen window and said, "Wow, Annie Bee. I should really shred that pasture if we want to store up any haybales for Nell this winter."

The glossy dumbness was gone from his eyes. Wonky Daddy wouldn't say such a thing, didn't think about shredding the pasture, and didn't call her Annie Bee. Normal Daddy was back. Drinking Molly's water must have cured his oogie head somehow, just like rubbing the egg over her ant bites and his turtle bite healed their skin.

She grabbed him tight, and her face went into his belly. He patted her back and rubbed the tender spot between her shoulder blades. She pulled away and looked into his face. He smiled, and the 'knowing' was there. He was cured for sure.

"Now shouldn't you be getting off to school?" he asked and bopped her nose with the tip of his finger.

She gripped his ears, and with raised eyebrows asked, "Dad? Is that really you?"

"Well of course it is. Who else would I be?" he asked and smiled into her eyes.

She didn't have to wait for the school bus today. It was there waiting for her as soon as she opened the front door. She looked back at Dad and grinned at him one last time before sprinting for the road.

The first day of Fifth grade was everything she'd hoped for. Her new teacher, Mrs. Martindale, had long, flowy, brown hair and she smelled like cinnamon rolls.

Her room smelled like oranges. It was clean, with stacks of books lining the back wall and a cozy little reading nook in the corner. She read to them for half an hour from an amazing new book about hunting dogs called, Where The Red Fern Grows.

Next, Annabelle was thrilled to find Mrs. Martindale's favorite subject was science, just like hers. Her brilliant new teacher handed them a science book with sea turtles and exotic fishes on the cover. Then she teased at all the wonderful experiments they would learn this year, like how airplanes fly, how the solar system worked, and even how to use potatoes to make a light bulb shine. Annabelle's imagination sparked with wonder, but still, somewhere at the back of her mind she worried Dad would go to the backyard and find Molly swimming in Nell's water trough.

Electric tingles crawled up her neck when Mrs. Martindale gave them an assignment at the end of the day. Write a one-page essay about what you did over summer break. Annabelle couldn't wait to get home to get started. She took her seat in the third row of the school bus and pulled out her new yellow spiral notebook. She flitted the pages with her thumb and savored the fresh smell. Then she pulled a pencil from her pouch and wrote:

My dad is special because this summer he died and came back to life. Our air conditioner stopped working, so he got his tools together and climbed into the attic to fix it. I went to the creek to go fishing and when I came back, I found him...

She left off there just as the school bus rounded the corner for Crabtree Road. She stood to look out the window, expecting to see Dad waiting at the mailbox for her. He wasn't there. She leaped down the bus steps and sprinted for their front porch, overjoyed to tell him all about Mrs. Martindale and her new classroom and the first day of fifth grade.

She dropped her backpack in the hallway, and her heart sank when she saw the attic stairs were lowered to the hardwood floor. A brown screwdriver rested under the lowest rung. The muscles in her throat tightened, and she tried to swallow. Dad's clunky boots were tied, and his legs were crossed over each other, but they didn't move.

She climbed the steps, and a familiar smell wafted to her. The stench of charred hair and electric ozone permeated the air all around. Dad's tools were scattered, and his face was like gray plastic. She knew he'd been that way for a long while and wasn't coming back.

The Whimpering
Seaton Kay-Smith

The smell of stale cigarettes and beer; the sound of music, indecipherable beyond the bass and percussion, bleeding through the thick concrete walls, painted black, faded, chipped; long faces, bloodshot eyes; looks of concern, worry, and fear.

I'd given them little notice and no explanation for my visit or the gathering, yet they have come all the same to a small underground pub in the middle of nowhere. It is cold outside and snowing. I gaze across the damp wooden table at my childhood friends and marvel at how old they have all become. It has been an age since we'd all been in the same room together, and that age is evident on every one of their tired, anxious faces.

'How many years has it been?' I think to ask, but don't.

I already know how many years it has been. I have counted them. I've spent the entire afternoon doing just that; standing in the cold, lips chapped, arms wrapped around me for warmth. I've thought of little else.

The flickering light of the electric candle creates shadows on the faces of my friends, accentuating the lines that run across them. 'Worry lines', I believe they're called. How many were added tonight, I wonder, when I'd asked them to meet me after so long a silence?

They barely touch their drinks. The mood is tense. They fidget and twitch, waiting for an explanation. It has been so long. Why now? Why this group? Friendships long thought dead and buried, suddenly dug up. They want to know why. Perhaps they want to know why there is dirt beneath my fingernails?

"Do you remember?" I ask.

They do not answer, holding their breath collectively.

"…when we were kids?"

Their brows furrow.

"…how we killed that thing?" I continue.

Still, they say nothing. They stare at me like I am a ghost—a cold patch of air, a shiver up their spine, static electricity making the hair on their arms dance and tingle. It is as though they think that if they blink, there is no guarantee that when they open their eyes, I will still be here.

"We were in the woods…" I say, hoping to remind them. The chipped and faded walls of our private room deadens the sound of my voice and robs it of an echo. The air is warm, stuffy, thick. The heater nearby is humming. Warmth, like a vaporous pearlescent forcefield is radiating off it. I shift my gaze back to my friends. "In the dark," I say.

Finally, one of my friends speaks. Amy. Her voice is barely breath, as though she has forgotten to attach vibrations to it. She draws out the word, 'Aaaaah' as she performs the theatre of searching her mind for a match. Then, finding none, she punctuates her 'ah' with a monosyllabic, "No."

The room is empty except for us. The bar beyond the long corridor is quiet. It's the middle of winter; the roads are icy. The only people out are the ones who have to be. I glance over my shoulder; the door is closed; we are alone.

"Remember, we were in the woods. We were playing spotlight… with our torches." My memory of the night is clear; my ability to communicate it clearly, is not. It is as though the words are shrouded in the same dark night as those woods, the same terrible, immemorial black. "The snow had melted—had started to. There were tufts of it, patches. The air was cold, but we didn't mind. We were kids… hot blooded, running around. It's funny," I say and almost laugh, "I can see the snow in my memory, but I we were all sweating. There was steam coming out of our mouths. Rising off our heads."

I turn to Tom, who instinctively diverts his gaze, sending it down and into the beer, barely touched, in front of him.

"Something moved in your beam of light," I tell him. "Remember? We went to investigate. That's when we found that thing. It was cowering beneath a fallen log: Light fur like peach fuzz over its olive-green body." The horrible memory flashes before my eyes, a vision of the creature, lurking in the shadows, hunched. "It would have been about the size of a cat, but it walked on two legs. Two long, elongated legs. It had a limp, remember, and it was shivering. It was…" I search for the word, "whimpering."

Tom is still looking down. His eyes continue to swim laps in his drink.

"You poked it with a stick, Tom. You were like, 'what the fuck is that?' And it was, like, batting the stick away with its three fingered hand. It was whimpering. The whole time, whimpering. And you just kept poking it and poking it. It obviously didn't like it. It was terrified. Then it kind of, just like, lashed out, I guess? Remember? Amy, you hit it with a rock."

Amy's eyes grow wide. She folds her arms across her chest and starts to mutter to herself, "Damian, I—"

"Its flesh was so soft," I say, "the rock almost got lodged in it. Or maybe the flesh wasn't soft. Maybe you just hit it so hard that… Soft or not, it got stuck there."

Their eyes on me, now, I can tell they're starting to remember. They listen quietly, mouths open, not so much breathing as allowing air to enter and exit their lungs discreetly. Every so often, they cast side-eyed glances at one another and swallow the thick glugs of saliva pooling at the back of their throats. Occasionally, I catch them checking the path to the door, making sure that it is free from obstruction. Perhaps they are counting in their heads the number of steps they'd have to take to get there. To get back to the main area of the pub, up the stairs and into the snow-covered streets outside. But I know they will not leave. If they were going to leave, they wouldn't have come at all.

"The whimpering got worse," I continue, "and its blood was black. We were all just standing around and looking at it, wondering 'what the hell is this thing?' Three fingers, black blood, soft downy fur like a peach— its olive-green body—always whimpering. Remember?" My gaze flicks to Tom. "You poked its wound. Poked it again and again. It didn't resist, didn't fight back, it just kind of lay there looking at us with its goat-like eyes, burning gold, glossy from tears. And you kind of moved the stick into the wound, and you kept pushing."

Tom's head begins to shake—back and forth, back and forth. The memory, no doubt, is hovering at the edges of his mind: The stick plunging deeper and deeper, the end of it slowly disappearing into the black-stained wound of the frightened creature at his feet. Back and forth, back and forth—his head is still shaking. Perpetual motion, perpetual denial.

"After the thing stopped moving, I nudged it with my foot. It spasmed. Scared the hell out of us, and Tom said, 'Don't kick it', and I said, 'I'm just seeing if it's still alive'. And I felt so resentful in that moment, how you'd told me off for that because, like, you'd literally just impaled it."

The look on Tom's face as he did it too. It was horrible. A child burning ants with a magnifying glass, pulling wings from a fly, emotionless, curious, dead eyed and soulless.

"That was the last time it moved… That spasm. It was quiet after that. Everything was. We were… The woods… Everything. The birds stopped screeching, the creek… Alone out there, abandoned, the sound gone, everything gone. No wind, either, I don't think. I knew it was dead, but I nudged it again with my foot. I don't know why, maybe to prove I wasn't kicking it, that I was just nudging it. How funny," I say, then lift my gaze again. Their faces are no longer expressionless. Their mouths have twisted into horror and shock. Eyes wide, brows tense. They were there. I do not understand why they seem so surprised.

"You don't remember that?"

As there was then, on that night so long ago, now too there is silence. The warping bass coming from the pub down the hallway, warbles, shaking the walls and door almost imperceptibly, muffled by thick concrete and heavy black paint. The murky sounds pulsate through the air around us, close in on us. An auditory vignette, gentle as it is, encroaching on our table, as if to frame us.

"You really don't remember?" I ask again. "You don't remember how we tried to dig a hole with the sticks so that we could bury it. But the ground was too hard—frosty—so we covered it in stones instead. Then used the sticks to make a wooden cross—a crucifix—a kind of tombstone type thing. We stuck it between the rocks."

Still, no one says a thing.

They were there. We all were. The five of us had stood there, hands in our pockets, necks slung low, heads heavy, full of fresh regret. We stared into the soil too hard to break through with sticks. The air had grown colder; we'd stopped moving. The evening frost; the winter not quite over. Myself, Amy, Saeed, Larissa, and Tom, full of remorse for what we had done, our mouths sewn shut with shame… Was there someone else?

"We didn't say anything. We just kind of stood there—" My hands are trembling; the memory of dirt still colors my palms. "—in silent vigil around the grave of that thing. The whimpering had come back. It had wormed its way through the cracks in our pitiful tower of rocks and stones and breaking the silence. The creature was dead, buried, but I could still hear it. You really don't remember? You don't remember the whimpering?"

I am there now, in my head. Beside the makeshift grave. Ten years old, yet somehow, no longer a child. My innocence lies buried beneath the topsoil, inelegantly drowning in dirt. The air, stale and stagnant, stifling despite the cold. Lip quivering, turning blue, eyes hot and wet with tears. Clothes damp—from snow, from sweat—turning icy in the chill of the night. Surrounded by friends, yet so incredibly alone.

Hungry, lost, full of shame.

I describe what I see: My memory—our memory. "We started to walk away, remember? Saeed, you were first, and we all just kind of followed, one by one. We didn't say anything, we just left. A silent procession, refusing to look one another in the eyes. Like a funeral march to the gallows—grieving, guilt-ridden… I was the last to leave. I was at the back… and… I don't think I ever told any of you this, but… before I left, I took the crucifix out. I thought that—I felt so much shame—I didn't want anyone to find it. I thought a crucifix, if someone came walking, they might get curious—they might dig through the rocks there. So, I took it out and broke it, then threw it into the woods. You really don't remember any of this?"

"No." Larissa says. The word, though small, falls heavily out of her mouth and lands with a dull thud on the table. The others just shake their heads.

"You don't remember going into the woods?"

No response.

"You don't remember going to the woods at all?"

Nothing.

"You don't remember camping, hiking, playing spotlight with our torches?" They hold their silence like a shield, "You don't remember the whimpering? I still hear the whimpering."

"I don't remember the whimpering," Tom snaps. He settles quickly when Amy places her hand on his forearm.

It wasn't a dream, or a nightmare." I was there. They were there… The world is spinning. I breathe deeply to steady myself and rest my hands on the edge of the table. "I went back to the woods," I tell them. "Back to where we always went. I found the grave."

"There is no grave," Tom says, shrugging his way out from under Amy's hand. He stares at me, holding my eyes in a death grip with his own, challenging me.

I accept his challenge. I have seen it, and recently. I know there is a grave. I have no need to fight for this truth. "I found the grave," I say, calmly, slowly, "…And I found its skeleton. Its skull had caved in. I don't know how much of that was us, or if, over time, the calcium became weak and the bones just kind of…crumpled. But it was there." I see it in my mind's eye, the yellow-grey bones, the dirt, the cracks, the dust. "…about the size of a cat. Barely buried beneath the stones. There were Mushrooms growing there. It's been so long, though, I don't think the mushrooms were feeding on the nutrients of that thing, but they were there. There wasn't much else, just… snow." I look up again, this time, I find Larissa's eyes. "You don't remember swimming in the stream in the summer? You don't remember playing hide and seek?"

"I remember swimming in a stream," Larissa says, her eyes now studying the small cardboard pyramid in front of her—the drinks specials.

"That was in these woods," I tell her.

"Are you sure? Because—"

"I… Yeah, yes." I was sure. "Anyway… I dug it up."

Silence engulfs us like a riptide, pulling us under, intent on drowning us. The silence, so loud, for a moment, it is all that I hear.

"What do you mean?" Saeed asks with a voice so soft, it's almost a whisper.

"I dug up the skeleton. Moved all the rocks away."

"Why?"

I shrug. "I don't know. I just started… At first, I wanted to know if I had remembered correctly. If what I remembered was real. Sometimes, it… I've been having these nightmares. I don't know what happens in them…"

Tom stares at Amy, then shoots his gaze in my direction. He leans over the table and hisses, "How do you know they're nightmares if you don't know what happens in them?"

"It's a feeling," I say. "I wake up drenched in sweat, exhausted. My muscles ache… And I'm… I feel so incredibly lonely, like I miss being me, even though I still am me. But am I the me I always was? Anyway… The feeling goes away, eventually, but it stays longer each morning. And in those dreams, I hear it: The whimpering. Footsteps through snow; children laughing, crying; soft flesh being punctured with sticks; the cracking of skulls beneath rocks. Sometimes, when I wake up, I guess my brain is still half asleep—half in our reality, half in the dream—and I hear it, piercing the walls of the morning: the whimpering. It's there. It's not coming from anywhere in particular, it's just, kind of, there. I thought if I dug up the creature, found out if it was real—if my memory was real, if the creature was—I thought I might find that it wasn't, and that I was just… I don't know… Anxious. But I'm not anxious. It's been fifteen years," I say, changing directions mid-sentence. "Longer. I haven't thought about the creature for a long time. I've lost so much weight; I thought I had cancer. I've been itchy, had these rashes. I thought it was lymphoma. I've been having these terrible headaches… There's nothing wrong with me," I assure them, clocking the concern on their faces, which I realize as I'm speaking, might not be for me so much as for themselves. "My white blood cell count is a bit lower than it should be, but there's nothing physically wrong with me.

"I put the skeleton in a plastic bag, then I tied it—I don't know why—I guess to stop it from falling out. It was a takeaway bag from that Chinese place. I don't know if it's still around; it was never very busy… Then, I put the bag in the boot and went home. The whole drive, there was this sound coming from the boot: a rattling… like, a clanging. Loose parts, or something… Clang, clang, clang. When I got home, that thing was still there, in the bag, tied up… The bones hadn't even moved around. I couldn't work out what had been making that sound. It wasn't the… Anyway… I didn't know what to do with the body, so I messaged you all. I wanted to—I guess, I wanted to see what you thought I should do, what you thought we should do. To, I don't know, make amends, plead for forgiveness. Have you been having the nightmares?"

"No," Larissa says, her voice stern, but with a distinct aftertaste of fear in it—metallic; bitter. "Damian, I don't remember any of this. There was no—I don't—"

Does she think I'm crazy?

"I don't remember anything," adds Saeed.

Tom says nothing. His eyes are closed again. Perhaps he is wishing he is elsewhere. That he hadn't come when I'd messaged him, that he was still at home, warm and comfortable, dry and safe. He had avoided us all for so long—for fifteen years—had ignored messages before… Of all times to cave to the pressure of an invite…

"Amy?" I ask. "What about you?"

Amy bites her lip. She stares at the table. They move slowly across it like she's reading the bumps, grooves and grains of it; the swollen circles where wet glasses had been placed without a coaster. She looks up. Her irises are almost non-existent—her eyes are pupils. "Where is the body now?" she asks.

I take the bag from my feet and place it on the table. It hits the beer-logged wood with a soft thud and a crinkling of plastic. The word 'YUM' is printed in a deep red. The capitalized letters are warped and faded.

"Jesus Christ," Tom says, finally breaking his silence. "What the fuck?" It's as though he's never seen a plastic bag. "Is that…" he stammers. "Is that it?"

I do not need to answer.

"Why the fuck did you bring it into the bar?"

"I don't know…to show you it?"

"Jesus," he says again. "People eat on this table."

"It's in a plastic bag," I say, defending myself. For a moment, I wonder if I've done the wrong thing. There is terror in each of their eyes. Worry lines etched deeply in their foreheads. Dread. Up till now, they have refused to remember. Perhaps, if they see the decay they're responsible for, their minds will open, and the memories locked inside, stubbornly repressed, will find freedom once more. Perhaps it will force them to face what they have done?

I untie the plastic handles and open it.

"Oh my God," one utters.

"What the fuck?" says another.

"It looks like a cat."

"The skull is completely pulverised," I explain, glancing at Amy, the one-time wielder of the rock. "What do you think we should do?"

"Put it back," says Tom.

"Back?" I do not know what he means.

"Bury it."

"Bury it?"

"Bury it," he says again.

"I just dug it up."

"Bury it. Say a few words if you need to, just get rid of it."

Keeping my eyes on him, I tie up the bag, then remove it from the table, and place it gently at my feet with my other things. "There's something else I need to tell you…"

"Something else?" Amy asks.

"Is someone going to say something?" Tom asks.

Larissa scolds him. "Tom."

"It looked like a fucking cat."

"Tom." She scolds him again.

"There's something else," I say again.

"For God's sake, what?" Tom asks, snapping his attention back to me.

"When I got home…I looked in the trunk. Like I said, it was still there, but something smelt…strange." They bristle at my words, faces contorting in disgust, as though the strange smell has somehow found its way into our private room in the underground pub. "I checked the bag, opened it, tied it back up. Nothing had changed. There was nothing in it apart from the bones and the still moist dirt dusting it. There was no reason for the odor as far as I could tell…and that's when I saw a glint, a reflection of light."

I close my eyes, and the memory comes at me like a speeding train—that glint, the light—a strike of lightning in a room as dark as pitch; a flashlight in the night, shining in my eyes; stunning daylight bursting through an opened door. "There was something else in there," I tell them. "Not in the bag, in the boot. It was another one of those things."

"What?" Amy and Saeed say, almost in unison.

"Another one of the creatures, I guess you'd call them. This one was lighter in color, like mustard, with the same peach fur, the same golden eyes. Goat eyes. This one wasn't whimpering. This one…was…stoic, I guess. It was just kind of looking at me from the darkness of the boot."

Their jaws hang open, the worry lines on their foreheads like fault lines—terrible tectonic plates, pushing together to make mountains of madness. Aging them further, it saps from them that small modicum of youth they'd been holding onto, prying it from their rapidly decomposing grips until I am no longer able to see the children I once knew in them. Scalps slowly rotting; the pigments dying; their brown, black, and red hair turning grey, falling out. Hearts withering, souls escaping through their mouths, wrapped in breath. They leave their bodies as vaporous plumes to dissipate in the thick humid air of the underground room.

"It scared the shit out of me," I admit. "Reflexively, I went to close the boot, but…then… I don't know what came over me… I stopped. I just kind of stood there… over it. I said I was sorry, sorry for what we did. So sorry. It was out there, all alone, it must have been so scared. 'I'm so sorry', I said. I don't know if it understood me, so, I leaned into the boot, pressing the palms of my hands against the back of my car. I wanted to get on the same level as the thing; to show it I wasn't a threat. I extended my hand so it could smell me… My hand."

I extend my hand in a facsimile of the moment.

"I figured, if it bit me, I deserved it. But it didn't bite me, it just… It flinched, then, kind of, shuffled back a bit, cautious. It smelled my hand as it looked at me and I could just tell   that something had changed."

"How?" Larissa asks.

"I could just tell. It was how it was looking at me. It's like curiosity was there, where only fear and anger had been. I beckoned it out of the boot, and it slinked forward, its elongated legs moving strangely—staccato almost— like every sixth frame had been dropped. It moved both slow and fast at the same time. And it…it kind of…it came out…and it looked at me… And this is going to sound crazy—"

"This whole thing sounds crazy," Tom almost shouts as he looks around the room, perhaps for someone outside our circle to validate his claim? No one does. No one even meets his eyes.

We are alone in a private room at the end of the corridor in an empty pub. There is no air in here that didn't come in with us. The streets are covered in snow, the air is frozen. There is no one out there for miles. Tom is sweating more than the others. His body shines, his musk fills the room. It is like his body is lubricating itself in the hope that doing so will aid its survival and allow him to slip away.

"This whole thing is crazy," he repeats, quieter now. "I wasn't there. It didn't happen—not like that. I don't remember it. You need help."

"I do," I say. "That's why I called you all here."

"Actual help," Tom says.

"Have you told anyone else about this?" Larissa asks.

"I wanted to tell you first. You were there."

"I wasn't there," Tom spits, muttering under his hot stinky breath, adding heat to air, already thick with it. Shoulders hunched, arms hanging limply. He is still wearing the jacket he came in with. His face is slick with sweat. His hair is plastered to his forehead. He speaks to me but refuses to raise his eyes. "I don't think you were there either," he sulks.

"I mean, it happened," I say. "I don't know what to tell you. I've got the bones here. They were where we left them. They were where you plunged a stick into it." I turn to Amy, "They were where you smashed its head in with a rock."

"Jesus Christ," Tom slides his hands over his sweaty brow and through his hair. Stretching his face, he creates a Greek mask of it—Melpomene, the muse of tragedy. "Why are you saying this? You disappear for fifteen years, send us all a message saying you had to see us urgently, bring us to this abandoned dive bar in the middle of nowhere… The weather is terrible, it's late, it's a weeknight… You drag us out here, and this is what you want to talk to us about? I thought—I shouldn't have come—"

"Tom," Larissa scolds.

"I have a kid. I paid for a babysitter."

"I'm just saying: it was there. It was where we left it."

Tom turns back to me. "I feel guilty, okay. I do. That's why I'm here. We shouldn't have left you in the woods that night, but it was a ten-minute walk home. We'd been running around. I didn't think about the cold or about any of that. We were kids. We didn't know you'd get lost for days. But this, this stuff with the dead cat? That never happened."

The bag crinkles at my feet, my foot brushing against. "This next thing is even crazier," I say.

"For fuck's sake." Tom squeezes his head in his hands.

"Because, when I was looking at it and it at me—the creature in my boot—I knew what it wanted. It was communicating with me, not with words but…with emotions? Like I was sharing its feelings. And it didn't feel good. It was sad, angry…disappointed. It wanted something."

"Did something happen in the woods, Damian, when you were out there?" Larissa asks, grabbing at my hands.

"Yes," I say, pulling them back. "We killed that creature."

"The babysitter charges $10 an hour. I'm leaving."

"We killed it, and the creature I found, wanted something from me…of me…"

Tom, standing now, stops, and turns around. Despite himself, he is listening.

"What did it want?" Larissa asks, trepidation in her voice, like her question is her hand and the answer is a flame. She wants me to speak, but she dreads what I will say. "What did it want?" she asks again, pushing her hand ever closer, forcing her body to act against its better judgement, ignoring her survival instincts, her fear of pain as she pushes her hand deeper into the fire.

"It wanted me to do something for it. To make up for what we'd done. To—not make things right—make things fair?"

"Fair?" Saeed asks.

"Balance the scales. It had…things."

"Things?" Saeed asks.

I can feel his heartbeat, his fear. "It had things with it in the boot."

"What do you…" Saeed's heartbeat gets louder. "What do you mean?" Ba boom. Ba boom. Ba boom.

"It's impossible," I admit.

"What did it have?" Larissa asks.

"It's impossible," I say again. "It's like it was the same stick."

Larissa leans forward, "The same stick?" Ba boom. Ba boom. Ba boom.

"That stick would have decomposed," Tom spits, his rage growing, threatening to erupt again. He towers of me, a river of lava coursing through his veins. He refuses to believe. He refuses to remember. "It's been fifteen years!"

I know how long it has been. "It looked exactly the same."

"Fucking—lots of sticks look like lots of other sticks. You're not going to be able to tell the difference between two sticks, okay?"

I cannot fathom why Tom is so angry. His words imply that he accepts there are multiple creatures. Why can he not accept there is a single stick?

"I'm telling you: it was the same stick. It was the same rock…"

While the others are silent, Tom continues to thrash about in the waves of his anger, struggling through the current, refusing to sink beneath it. He kicks frantically, trying to appear calm while the water churns beneath him.

"This is fucking ridiculous. If you don't want to tell us what happened, fine. That's up to you. But, for what it's worth, I'm sorry, okay? I'm sorry we left you out there, but we were kids. When you turned up three days later covered in cuts and bruises, shivering… I—I'm sorry, okay? But this isn't healthy."

His movements emit a pulse. Electronic signals, like beacons, drawing me to him. It is as though I am a shark. "It was the same stick, the same rock," I say again. "It picked them up and handed them to me, and I knew what it wanted."

Ba boom. Ba boom.

Aside from Saeed's beating heart, the room is almost silent. The room still smells of stale beer and old cigarettes, bass still bleeds through the walls, but we are no longer in the pub. We are in a void of memory. The black hole of our past, sucking us in and trapping us, holding us in its icy grip.

Ba boom. Ba boom.

There is another face there now, in my memory, an older, crueler face. I flutter my eyelids, and it is gone.

"Why is the door locked?" Tom asks, bringing me back into the room.

He seems unwell, panicked.

Ba boom. Ba boom.

My right-hand rests on the table. My left, hidden, hangs beneath it, clutching the rock. I'm not even sure when I picked it up

The whimpering has returned.

The others are looking at me, as though they can hear it too. They are staring at me. Do they think the whimpering is coming from me? Soft scared sobs, like a child's, crying, sucking in air, face red, whimpering… Am I dreaming?

The whimpering gets louder, louder. It builds and grows, throbbing, pulsing, then stops as a warm hand, clammy, wet, and sticky with sweat, takes hold of mine.

Beneath the table, with my other hand, I squeeze the rock. Sand crumbles to the floor. My hands are shaking—my whole body.

Amy is staring at me, closer than I'd thought. Her face is blank; the lines are gone. Her heart is audibly beating. It rattles around in her ribcage, but, despite this, she is still—eyes wide, apologetic, sad. It is like she has let go of all her confusion and disbelief; her refusal to remember. Her seeming acceptance of the truth, stripping away the layers of age which have piled onto her over the past fifteen years. The guilt and shame, heavy, crushing her spirit, snuffing her flame; they are gone now, and for a moment, she's the girl I used to know, who I'd play hide and seek with, and spotlight, splashing through the stream in the warmer months.

Ba boom. Ba boom.

She is young again, innocent, like she was before that night in the woods, when the whimpering began. To go back there… to go back there… I want to go back. I flex my fingers around the rock, digging in, biting down. I cannot make things right, but I can make them fair.

Ba boom. Ba boom.

I can balance the scales.

Ba boom. Ba boom.

"Damian," she says, her hand still resting on mine. Her flesh is soft, the hairs on her arms, light, like peach fuzz…

Ba boom. Ba boom.

"…why did you ask us here?"

The Stench

Milan Kovačević

Gary had been peering through the musty windshield for over twenty minutes. The wipers screamed across the glass, revealing just enough for him to scowl at what lay ahead. He was muttering to himself, while gritting his teeth, about all the things that had brought him to where he was; and there had been many of those, too many to recall them all. He sat, smoking cigarette after cigarette, occasionally spitting through the half-open car window. His jaw clenched, words spilling under his breath – bits of regret, anger, unfinished thoughts – like ash from the cigarettes piling at his feet.

When he ran out of plows, he squashed the box and dropped it at his feet. The crumpled paper landed near the clutch, among waste of every kind: cans, drool wipes, and parking tickets from all around the state. The old bronze Chrysler had been serving him well enough, although the tank was nearly empty, and the seat covers smelled of sweat and tobacco. This is supposed to be the last job. But as it usually goes, things backfired. And this shot hit him right between the eyes.

After several hours of hard driving, he was in the backwoods at the borders of Georgia, under the night sky, away from all his old problems, facing only a specific new one. The day had long since passed, and the night descended with a biting cold that gnawed at his very marrow. In front of him lay a swampy landscape that looked as if no human had passed through it in centuries.

While in prison, he'd heard stories from other inmates who used to live in the area, about some national park or other, but he was convinced that such an overgrown abomination couldn't carry the name of anything significant. In fact, he chose this place precisely because he wouldn't encounter another human being. Anyone with half an ounce of brain wouldn't spend a single minute here. And if the wrinkled map he kept propped up next to his seat was to be believed, they had bypassed all the natural landmarks in the area. That was another thing he'd learned from the other prisoners: this beloved country is full of places that devour ugly truths and misdemeanors.

"Shit. I'm out of cigs," he said.

"I think that's the least of the fuckin' problem," said Mike, who—until then—had sat silently in the passenger seat. He was too young for such things; not sufficiently ruined by bad living; or that's just what Gary thought, as an old-school mobster.

"Shut your fuckin' muzzle," Gary shouted, "...I'm thinkin'."

"Do you see where your thinking has landed us?" Mike asked, then pulled a half-empty packet of Lucky Strike from his pocket.

"It was a damn accident. You know that." Gary grabbed another cigarette.

"I know, but how are we going to explain it to Mr. Murray?" Mike asked, then opened the door to get some air. "Shit. This place stinks like hell."

Another cigarette butt was thrown out the window. Gary took a flask from the compartment in the door and poured the warm cheap liquid down his throat. He coughed, then licked the lower part of his thin mustache.

"Close the door, it's getting colder," he said.

"Where are we, anyway?"

"If the map is to be believed, we are somewhere near the good ol' Sunshine State. Once we get rid of this load, I think we should go farther south. I know a guy growing some decent herbs somewhere near Limestone. He'll give us a place to stay. He owes me, for some shit I took care of a long time ago."

"And Mr. Murray?" asked Mike.

"To hell with him. I've had enough of crawling up that old bastard's ass."

"Maybe we should call him and try to explain what happened," said the younger man, putting his fists above his forehead.

He had some kind of inscription tattooed on his fingers; the name of the street where he grew up or some gibberish slogan. Gary never liked tattoos, especially when they were in visible places and had as much significance as traffic lights in the desert.

"Yeah, you could try that, but don't call me when the old man slits your tits and drowns you in his private piranha pool. Admit it, kid, we're screwed. Whatever we do, calling the old prick is not a good option."

Mike fell silent again. He reached for the flask to wet his dry throat. Gary was right, as much as he didn't want to admit it to himself. They were two dead men in an old rusty car; probably lost and on the run. Actually–there were three of them there. But only one–at least at the time–was truly dead. Mike looked in the rearview mirror, and his gaze returned to the corpse, already deprived of life for several hours. A skinny guy in his thirties, with a meaty hollow in his skull. They were too hasty–all they needed to do was intimidate the debtor and find out where all of Mr. Murray's cash had gone. The secret was now lost forever, and their boss didn't like to hear bad news.

"When we drink this, we go. We'll throw the wretch in the swamp, then we'll launch south, and be done with these crappy lives," said Gary.

"Do we have any kind of lamp?"

"Don't think so. But I have a damn good fake Zippo, and the headlights should light the road well enough."

"Road?" Mike asked, "I don't see any road."

"It's just a figure of speech, you dumb-fuck."

The marsh, under the cloak of nighttime, took on a foreboding atmosphere. The silhouettes of twisted, gnarled trees loomed like ancient sentinels, their branches swaying softly in the chill breeze that rustled the dying reeds. The moon, shrouded by a veil of thin clouds, cast a feeble glow over the muddy landscape, barely illuminating the murky water that lay at the fore. When they drained the last drop from the flask, they staggered out of the car, stretched their legs, and Gary went to take a leak. Only a few feet from the car, the ground was already wetter and softer, so that his boots sank slightly into the surface. His socks soaked up the cold dew from the marsh grass.

"Wonderful," he said, as he pulled his boots from the mud. "If we're lucky enough, the earth will swallow the kiddo by morning."

"What about the alligators?" asked Mike.

"Did you see one already?"

"Well, no."

"Then there's no need to worry or summon any bad juju. Now, help me out."

The air in front of them was thick with a haunting fog that rolled in from the swamp, obscuring everything in its path. It was the kind of mist that seemed to materialize from the very essence of the marsh itself. Lonely, most definitely forgotten, but alive in its own right. The wisps of fog danced around the car, casting eerie and shifting shadows.

Gary returned to the Chrysler and opened the back doors. The corpse was cold, somehow bleak, with a swollen tongue sticking out of its wide-open mouth. He pushed it toward the exit with his dirty boot, and the cadaver tumbled over the seat, hitting its head on the soft ground with its legs still in the car. Mike pulled the corpse by the collar, and after a little struggle, the body was finally out of the vehicle, stretched out on the dewy grass.

"That's more like it," Gary said.

They carried their load in front of the car and stood over it, panting. Gary turned on the high beams, leaving the car running. Translucent smoke collided with thick rays of light. In the distance–illuminated by the light–a dense row of pine trees and bald cypresses emerged from the muddy water, giving the impression of a huge living labyrinth. A few mosquitoes and other swamp critters began to zoom around the headlights. Mike grabbed the dead man by the arms, and Gary took hold of both legs. They wobbled a few meters or so when they realized that the terrain in front of them wouldn't support their weight.

"Watch your step!" cried Gary, as Mike lost his balance.

"It's not worth it. We'll snuff it like this. Throw him here," Mike yelled.

"Are you nuts? Even if this is a god-forsaken hole, we can't leave him on the glade. Maybe some crazy nature-loving motherfuckers will find him before dawn: hikers, bikers, those kinds of pricks. I know, the chances of that are pretty low, but why gamble? We're leaving, but only when this fella hits the bottom of this crap ocean. So, keep going."

"You are one crazy bastard, you know that?" Mike said.

"Yeah, I know. And it's not because of fuckin' Murray, believe me. I'm not going back to that dungeon. Fuck 'em."

"Remind me, how did you end up behind bars?"

"I think this is the worst possible time for any kind of sentimental chit-chat. But, long story short, I did something similar," Gary said, while pointing with his eyes to the dead body.

"So, this wasn't your first time?" asked Mike.

"No. It wasn't. Not even the second. But that fucker I smoked ten years ago, he was the only one who deserved it. Then came prison, and the rest is history... And this is history, dragging this fucker through the mud with you. Satisfied? Anyway, what's your story?"

"Well, just a regular one. Fucked up family. Fucked up neighborhood. A classic west-side tale. Some weed dealin', some penitentiary. Then I came across one hoodlum who worked for Mr. Murray, and he hooked me up with one of the generals, as they used to call 'em. I actually never saw the old man."

"Well, I saw him, and everything you've heard is true. The truth is–if I may say–even worse. But worry not. We're out of that shit job. When we get to Limestone... well, you'll see."

The mud and water were above their ankles, and the marsh grass slowed them with every sluggish step. It was already past midnight, and tingling followed the upcoming witching hour, which made the skin of the two men crawl. Mike sloppily let go of one of the dead man's arms and began to scratch the back of his neck.

"Damn bugs! They're everywhere," he shouted.

"Just a bit more. Keep your head up." said Gary.

They were breathing heavily. Although the dead young man was skinny, it wasn't an easy task to drag a stiff body through such hostile terrain. Soon they stopped talking; they were already too tired to waste their energy on idle chatter. The light provided by the car was slowly fading, and most of the visibility was due to its reflection on the watery surface on which they walked. The only sounds they heard were the buzzing of mosquitoes and the churning of mud as it collided with their exhausted legs. The burden they were carrying was getting heavier, and their hands were losing strength. Their fingers trembled manically as the they squeezed the corpse's limbs.

They stopped looking each other in the eyes, aware of the shameful work they were doing. Whenever one would raise his head, the other would lower it. They had reached–by tacit agreement–the bottom. Mike believed Gary's story about the marijuana field near Limestone, but the question was, did Gary even believe it, knowing that he had always been a good liar? Maybe too good, for his own sake. That was, after all, a distant possibility. A tool to make things easier for Mike. Gary liked his companion; he reminded him of his younger self. He wanted, if possible, to ease the situation in which they found themselves.

This stupid kid shouldn't have died, they both thought, like their minds were connected. There are too many scoundrels in the world who must have done far worse things, and there they were, alive and well, sipping cocktails in their private gardens. And this kid borrowed some money, tripled it, but soon, as it usually goes, lost everything.

So, he borrowed twice as much, magically disappearing after that. The money wasn't lost, it was–as the boy had said–in a safe place. Too bad the location disappeared with him. The cash could be anywhere; there were so many places suitable for hiding things. They were just crossing one of them–the foggy marshland, home of no one.

The atmosphere was thick with a strange smell neither of them had ever encountered before. The insects retreated, and their night song stopped. The stench was a ghastly combination of rotting vegetation, putrid water, and something altogether unnatural. It clung to the air alongside a sinister fog, suffusing the atmosphere with an unsettling, otherworldly aroma.

"...the fuck is this stink?" asked Gary.

"I don't know, but it certainly drove off the bloodsuckers."

"Look over there." The older man pointed in the darkness with his eyes. "That's the spot."

In the heart of the wretched swamp slept a small, desolate patch of dry land; an island of withered grass and gnarled trees that clawed at the sky like skeletal fingers. As the moon's feeble light barely penetrated the canopy of twisted branches, this forsaken oasis amid the swamp seemed to be a perfect place for disposal.

"Are you sure?"

"Yeah, I'm sure. The terrain kinda slopes behind it, which means the real depths are just a couple of yards beyond. Help me toss this buddy on it."

As they reached the small elevation and lifted the corpse onto it, they climbed to a dry area bordered by strange vegetation and an even stranger odor. In the middle of the minuscule aisle, there was a little spherical object that resembled the top of a garden torch. It was made of woven pliable twigs and a foul stench emanated from the small hole on the top of it.

Gary walked up to the unknown thing and kicked it toward the water. Its fall was followed by a tiny splash, and everything went quiet as soon as the water calmed.

"Listen..." said Gary. "Nothing. This surely is some fucked up natural dereliction."

"I wonder how all of this looks in the daylight. This is so calm. Almost relaxing in a way."

"Feel free to check tomorrow, you stupid." Gary smiled. 'So... One, two, three?"

"One–two–three," they yelled at the same time and pushed the body from the ledge into the black water.

The deceased's face stayed above the surface for about fifty seconds as if he was staring pitifully at his executioners. Gary crouched and held the lighter to the face of the man they'd killed, waiting for him to sink. A blue tongue was still sticking out of the gaping mouth, but this time the teeth were deeply sunk into it. He stared at it for a few more moments, and the expression on the dead man's face suggested he was undergoing some kind of convulsion.

"He smiled..." he whispered to himself. "The bastard smiled," Gary said louder.

Mike—lost in some kind of strange sensation—studied the branches that towered over them, ignoring his colleague's words. His gaze wandered from one branch to another, with the strips of weak moonlight hitting the center of his widened pupils.

Gary turned his gaze toward Mike, wondering if everything was all right in his pulsating head. He recalled the alcohol he'd had earlier, but booze never made him see something that wasn't in front of him. Of course, that didn't apply to the old courtesans he lashed out at whenever he got wasted at some bar in Atlanta. They always seemed younger than they really were and more beautiful than they would ever be. However, the water swallowed yet another secret.

Gary stood up, lighter in hand. He calmly asked Mike for another cigarette–one for a job well done. The young man handed him the cigarettes, still gazing up. Gary bit down on the filter, brought a flame to the tip of the cig, and the space in front of him lit up just enough for him to see something he didn't expect.

"What the fuck is that..." The words leaked from his mouth.

"What?" asked Mike, while the high beams flashed twice from the direction they'd come from. He swiveled, yanked from the strange hypnosis. 'The car battery is dying!'

"What...the…fuck..." said Gary, ignoring the car they had left in the distance.

Mike squinted, trying to see what Gary was talking about. And somehow, he managed to glimpse a tall evanescent figure in the deep darkness, standing motionless and peering at them; a witness to the crime they'd just committed.

He wasn't sure if it was a human or an apparition with humanoid features. All he knew was that they'd been seen. And just as he was about to roar and call out to the creature that had appeared out of nowhere not far from them, the being started running into the opaque darkness beyond. Seeing just a little of what was in front of them, they were certain that the being was moving on some kind of wooden planks, laid above the water. The dull sound of bare feet hitting wet wood broke the silence of the swampy night.

"Hey! Stop there!" Mike screamed.

"Did you see it..." Gary said and grabbed Mike by the hand.

"Not sure, but he clearly saw us, and you know what that means."

"He? It's not a he. I saw a glimpse of the face... It is not a he."

"Then what is it?" asked Mike.

"Dunno. But, but... We should just go back to the car," said Gary.

"Listen up, old man. You're the tough one here, ain't you? Someone saw what we just did, and there's no way I'm going anywhere until I find that son of a bitch and make him take everything with him to the grave. There's no going back now, right?"

"Well...well, you're right. But something isn't right.' His eyes widened with sheer terror, as the strange smell yet again coursed through his nostrils, sending him into a disoriented, nightmarish whirlwind of dizziness "It's... It's that smell. It drove away the mosquitoes. And that thing showed up just after we noticed it... It's playing with our heads somehow."

"You're just not used to hard drugs, old fella, and this isn't one of 'em. But... I think you have a point. We should follow that stench."

"Screw you, kid. I wouldn't do this, but I'm sure that kid from the west side doesn't have bigger balls than me. And... I ain't going back without you. Whoa," Gary said, as he grabbed at the air in front of his face, trying to catch something that wasn't there.

Something is definitely not right, Gary thought, and Mike read his mind in an instant. They faced each other, this time looking into the other's eyes. They both stared for quite some time, watching how the sockets clustered then hastily imploded to normality again.

The eyes–which are often the windows to one's soul–had become swirling vortexes of endless darkness, with a need to draw the watcher into a realm of pure, unadulterated dread. The pupils expanded and contracted wildly, filled with a dark palette of surrounding colors.

"What's happening?" Gary asked, and his voice sounded like it was coming from someone else's mouth.

"We need to find that guy," Mike replied, slowly letting the sentences roll off his tongue. Their reality had turned into a classic silent film, played through a broken projector in juxtaposition.

Nevertheless, they somehow understood what they needed to do, so they set off decisively.

First, they jumped into the swamp where they'd thrown the corpse. It seemed the bottom had already swallowed him, or the water had taken him somewhere, which was strange because the surface was calmer than the pulse of someone long dead.

The water was now up to their waists. They were wading their way through the overgrown water lilies. These plants were a grotesque aberration, their blossoms resembling twisted, ashen genitals, clawing their way out of the muck, with each petal dripping with an iridescent ooze that seemed to pulse with an unsettling, otherworldly energy.

Gary twirled on his axis several times, kicking the muddy bottom, to make sure that the corpse had touched the sludge. But he felt nothing, except for the soft and hungry bottom. Several times he thought that someone was grabbing his leg, but he got rid of those thoughts, comforting himself that this was all just a terrible trip. He had always hated psychedelics, and as a descendant of full-blown hippies, he believed he had good enough reason.

When they reached the place where the witness was standing and climbed up to it, they walked under the light of the lighter, and after a couple of yards, they saw a long system of wooden plank bridges stretching before them, leading into the unknown. They headed across the first bridge, made of rotten boards, wide enough for one grown man to tread over. Soon, they found themselves in a stinking maze made of unknown vegetation, with several possible paths each leading in a different direction.

"Fuck, man. Where now?" Mike asked, as the network of bridges rippled before his eyes.

"You wanted to do this, so you take the lead. I'm kinda too old for this shit. I ain't no son of botanists either, or an explorer. And I think that I'm high as fuck. Actually, I can't feel my upper legs."

"I feel it too. It's getting stronger, the stench. Kinda dizzy, but that means we're on the right track. I can just assume that some crazy weed-druid lives here and now is going to die because he saw what he shouldn't have."

Gary laughed. That was a good one. But more than for a joke, he hoped that it was the final truth. Because if it's not true–he knew deep inside–they'd never leave this swamp alive.

As the strange drug started to take hold, reality fractured into a kaleidoscope of disorienting colors and shapes, and a profound sense of dread crept over them like an inescapable, creeping bad dream. Their limbs were propelled by an unholy compulsion, every step into the swirling darkness akin to a descent into madness, with the oppressive weight of dread pressing upon their hearts.

And still, an irresistible need to chortle clawed at their throats, but the laughter that bubbled forth was a nightmarish cacophony, hollow and mirthless, echoing through the swamp, like the deranged cackling of long-locked-up lunatics. They wandered, like blind dogs, occasionally grinning at nothing, gazing more at their feet than at the path they were walking on.

Soon, they realized that they'd separated. Mike was on a wooden bridge a few feet from the dirty water, while Gary was holding onto some soft stems through which another bridge made of weak boards passed. When he looked down, he saw only blackness. The deep night below him mirrored the black skies, where dark clouds now obscured the moon. On the other side, Gary held up his fake Zippo, but the flame at its tip was fading.

"No, don't disappear! A little more; just a little more," he said, but the light vanished.

In the heart of the unforgiving swamp, Mike and Gary found themselves immersed in a disorienting and relentless darkness. In this harrowing abyss, they were gripped by a profound dread, unable to shake the overwhelming fear that something sinister lurked just beyond their senses, forcing them to confront the horrifying unknown in a world where the relentless darkness was their only reality. They no longer saw the headlights of the Chrysler in the distance. Their only landmark has evaporated. Even the laughter, painfully infectious, stopped.

"Kid, I don't think we're going to make it out of here alive. This drug is tearing me a brand-new butthole. It's like my ass is where my head used to be, and vise versa. At least you won't see old Mr. Murray," Gary said, as he fake-laughed for the last time.

"Shut up, old man. Try to fight this. Think of something nice. Convince yourself that you're not out of your mind," Mike said, knowing he was fighting the same battle inside.

"I tried, believe me, I tried. But the more I resist, the more I feel like it's drowning me in madness. And, you know when you asked me why I ended up in jail? Maybe, well... Maybe I can tell you."

"You'll tell me when we get out of here. Now, let's meet on the central bridge, and be careful not to fall," said Mike.

In a few steps, Mike found himself at the agreed spot. Gary–on the other hand–was trying to regain his balance by treading tiny steps on the thin boards. He spread his arms like a retired acrobat in a failed circus, sliding forward inch by inch.

"I don't think I'll make it..." he said.

"Shut up, and keep going," Mike said. "Breathe."

In complete silence, Gary heard his own breathing. It was slow, deep, and labored. He looked ahead at Mike, who was waiting for him with open arms. Gary knew that he mustn't gaze down, because below him lay a swamp as black as tar, its depths home to monsters with names yet to be invented. At least that's how he imagined the darkness, into which he had thrown the lifeless body of a boy. His forehead prickled with moisture; a bead of sweat stung his eye as it slid down his temple. A few more steps. Just a few more.

The silence of the night was broken by a plank cracking. It snapped in half in the blink of an eye, and Gary found himself in free fall. He didn't even have time to scream, to say any last words, to ask God for forgiveness. Mike's hand flew toward him, their fingers barely touching; but that was all–the end. The man fell into the swamp, as dark as night, and was swallowed as soon as he hit the black surface.

"Gary," Mike yelled, but no answer came.

The trip would be marred by tragedy. As pushy and reckless as Gary was at times, he was one of the few people Mike called a friend. He was a father figure to him, and as bad as that sounds; he was better than Mike's real father, whom Mike had never even met. Now he was alone. And it was hard for him. Much harder than when Gary was around. Although he hadn't had much help from the old fella, even hell was a bit nicer if you're among your own.

He walked toward the darkness, knowing there was no turning back. More than once, he thought of taking his own life, to end this awful episode–in which he was forced to play–for good. But what's the point? If he'd lasted this long, he was going to push to the end, whatever it might be.

Just then, he seemed to see a flickering light in the distance. A gentle smoldering fire, or something like that. Deprived of strength, he staggered in the direction of the light. Now he was on the widest plank that was thick and seemingly connected a network of these rotten bridges to some kind of clearing. For the first time since they threw the unfortunate man into the water, he found himself on land that was made of solid earth. So, when he stepped onto the path of light, he was unaware he'd crossed into otherworldly territory.

A pyre was burning in the middle of the clearing, with a large stake protruding from its center. In the eerie glow of the flickering fire, beings shrouded in black cloaks moved in macabre unison. Their movements were a grotesque dance for the glory of something Mike couldn't recognize at first sight. The silhouettes jumped ominously against the fiery backdrop, with their faces obscured by shadow. They pretended he wasn't there as if the fact that he'd wandered into their little show didn't make a big difference. He searched for the knife he always kept tucked into his belt, but his fingers found nothing. It must have fallen out while he was making his way through the thick mud. Even if he did have it in his hands, what would he do with it? What could a tiny blade do to at least thirty beings spinning in ritual ecstasy in front of him?

His jaw went numb when he realized what was on the stake. That hollow in the head and the thin pale body; he would never forget them. This time his mouth was wide open, and his tongue was cut off at the root. He was smeared with some kind of strange-smelling oil, and an atypical cut and bad spindle stitches could be seen on his stomach.

He hovered over the fire but didn't burn; filled with something unknown, just like a stuffed toy. Then, one of the black figures approached the fire, bowed to the blaze and the altar, and began to speak, in a language Mike had never heard. As if summoned by a strange song, smoke billowed from the dead man's mouth. A smoke of putrid stench, similar to the one Mike inhaled earlier, but more intense and–in a way–more alive. The beings stopped their dance when the smoke surrounded them, turned toward the fumes, and began to inhale it with every part of their bodies. It was as if the smoke wasn't only clinging to their hidden faces but also to their hands, and their bare feet, as well.

The disgusting fumes also crawled in Mike's direction, and he covered his mouth with his hand as if he wasn't already drugged enough. He moved deeper into the center of the ungodly event, realizing he had nothing to lose. The stench was unbearable, but curiosity prevailed, especially combined with the intoxicating smoke that clung to his body.

He approached one of the apostles of stench, sneaked up to him from behind, grabbed his robe, and tore it off his figure with one powerful movement. What awaited him beneath pushed the entire contents of his stomach up and out through his mouth. What had once been a man was now a polluted humanoid anatomy, with burned skin and hundreds of strange burgeons. Some kinds of withered buds covered the disfigured skin, and nets of burning viridescent capillaries were pounding, like a slime river was running through them. Mike sighed, realizing that the poison was coming from the skin of these heathen freaks.

It grew, in the shape of some kind of unseen blossom, for sure; but they were off the blooming season. So, a vessel? He once again looked at the fuming carcass.

Finally, he heard the voices of these creatures. The uncovered one screamed into his face, and the sound was anything but human. Like a broken air raid siren. Only sharper, delivered through vocal cords destroyed by the inhaling.

The other beings also turned to Mike; the ritual had clearly been interrupted by an uninvited guest. This was the end of the road, but then he saw a piece of wood emerging from the fire. A solid stick, of which he knew not the origin, but good enough for his desperate move…

Like a rugby player, he lunged forward, forcing his way through the freakish creatures. Dust exploded beneath him as he hurled himself to the ground, reaching for the much-needed torch. Face down, vulnerable, with two swamp dwellers looming above, he twisted just in time, flame in hand, and set their robes ablaze.

Terrible screams filled the clearing yet again. The others stirred, giving Mike enough time to head for the wooden bridges he'd already crossed. This time, he had a torch in his hands, so the darkness couldn't be impenetrable.

His terror-fueled footsteps echoed across the rickety, wooden bridges suspended above the murky swamp waters. His heart raced, and cold sweat coated his trembling body as he fled from the grotesque beings that pursued him relentlessly.

The torch's feeble light was barely enough to pierce the oppressive darkness that surrounded him. The gnarled roots of ancient trees clawed at his feet as he navigated the labyrinthine network of bridges, their crooked paths and the gaps between the planks forcing him to balance on the edge of a precipice.'

The creatures' guttural, inhuman cries echoed through the night, their presence supported by the swamp's horrid echo. With every fleeting glimpse of their twisted figures, his dread deepened, and the pursuit grew ruthless. Each step he took was a desperate bid for survival in this nightmarish chase, his wooden torch casting an uncertain glow on the crooked path ahead. He glanced over his shoulder, realizing he was within their reach. Among the hounds were the two whose cloaks he'd burned. Hardy bastards.

The torch burned down. The embers at the top of the log were slowly dying. And just when he thought that all that effort had been in vain, he heard a familiar voice.

"Kiddo! Over here!" said Gary. He was standing on the first small aisle they'd encountered.

"You bastard! You're alive," Mike yelled as he rushed toward him.

"I'm too tough for my own good, son!"

"Run! Run, you bloody fool," Mike nearly tore his throat screaming.

"No. No more running," said Gary, more to himself, than to anyone else.

He had a knife in his hand and was ready for what was coming after Mike. It didn't matter to him. There was no one waiting for him in Limestone. It was just a white lie, but–since lies had been exposed–he won't have to make up any excuses. Mike ran past him, tears welling up in his eyes. He knew he couldn't persuade the old man to run. It's not that Gary was a brave man or a rumbler; he'd just made a choice a long time ago. Someone had to stay. In stories like this, tandems never survived. It would be too good to be true.

"Come on, shitheads," Gary said calmly, clutching the knife.

Mike was already in the shallow water, clawing his way to the car. He didn't look back, and all he heard was a human scream, so loud it overpowered the monster's roar. A thunderous crunching and breaking of bones followed him to dry land.

Everything was overrun with mosquitoes and other bugs again. The pests started sucking on Mike, but as soon as they took their required dose, they'd fall dead to the ground. There was no more putrid stench in the air, just the regular stink of the swamp. But the stench Mike would never forget—the derivative of a plant that grows on the faulty skin of swamp demons had vanished.

He finally reached the dead car and turned around. The creatures stood at the edge of the water, not moving any farther toward him. At their crooked feet were a mutilated body, disfigured and half-consumed. That was the border, he knew. They would never leave their native clod. Their roots were too deep, and time had come for him to plant his own somewhere. Far away from here, from this life.

A lump rose in his throat. He pictured a porch that never existed, voices he'd never heard, a warmth he only imagined in childhood dreams. It's time for things to change. From the edge of the swamp, he was still watched by once-human eyes, seared by the poisonous stench that kept them forever imprisoned in the heart of the marsh.

He got into the car but couldn't start the engine. Staying there was not an option. Dirty, wet, and tired, he decided to leave on foot. He took a map and the flask, and from the latter, he squeezed a single drop onto his tongue.

It was ten miles to the nearest highway, through meadow and pasture. And when he'd walked half of that, he came to a dirt road that led to the carriageway. His mouth was dry, and he couldn't catch a breath. Each breath came with a rasp, sharp and raw, as if tiny needles scraped the inside of his lungs. He clutched his chest, coughing dryly, the air itself biting back harder than any smoke he'd ever inhaled.

I breathed in the stench. He was kept alive by a desire for change, because only the living can seek betterment. He would forgive himself. And he'd seek forgiveness from all those he'd neglected and left behind.

The last shadows of the night were just beginning to fade as a faint glow flickered at the edge of the road—two headlights cutting slowly through the dark, growing brighter with each passing moment. A car was approaching. Far away, the sun had begun to rise. He raised his hand, hoping to stop the oncoming car. The black Mercedes halted, and the driver rolled down the window.

"Where to, my friend?" asked the driver eagerly.

"Help me... We had an accident. My friend and I... He is... Can you take me to the nearest city, please?" said Mike, already half-dead and sickly.

"That friend's name...was it Gary?" the driver asked, and rose from his seat, looking at the wounded hands of the exhausted young man. The old, engraved ink on his fingers was stained with blood but still visible.

"How... No, no, it wasn't," Mike said, though it was already too late.

"Mr. Murray sends his regards."

The driver took a gun out of his lapel. It was a decent caliber, one that could kill large game without causing too much suffering. A loud shot tore through the air. Birds flew out of the tops of nearby trees. The body of a young man was left lying in the dust. The car turned and drove away in the direction of the rising sun.

The Seraph in the Crawlspace
Julien Jayus

2 KINGS 2:12
> *And when he saw it, he cried, My father, my father,*
> *the chariot of Israel, and the horsemen thereof. And he*
> *saw him no more: and he took hold of his own clothes,*
> *and rent them in two pieces.*

Elisha Williams lay very still in the thick, teeming darkness that seemed to breathe and pulse around him, as though he lay in the stomach of some horrible beast. At eleven and a half years old, he was too old to be scared of the dark, or so his mother told him. So petrified was he of the creaking walk down the stairs to the bathroom that he would rather wet the bed than brave it by himself. His mother had yelled at him last time he'd done it. He was even worried she'd hit him. She'd never raised a hand against him or his sister in their lives, but for a moment he thought he saw a flash of it in her eyes and he flinched at it, which made her even angrier.

"Look," she'd said, once her anger had subsided from a boil to a simmer

She thrust her index finger at the wood-paneled hallway glowing with the golden midday sun streaking in sideways through his bedroom door ajar at the end of it. She stabbed the same finger at the worn carpeted stairs, at the family portraits that hung adjacent, smiling at him through the thin film of dust.

"There isn't anything there at night that isn't there now."

But there is! Elisha wanted to protest. *There's something here! I can feel it!* His traitorous heart raced in his chest. Under cover of night, the house was transformed in some unspeakable way. The hall: sheathed in shadow, stretching on indefinitely. The stairs: not as they were before. The portraits: the leering faces of strangers.

The darkness stirred, sensing his fear. Without opening his eyes, he knew that whatever lay hunched and waiting in the tenebrous corner of his room was unspooling itself and crawling toward the scent of his sweat. He could see it clear as day in his mind's eye as the thing unfurled a jagged claw, ready to plunge its blood-crusted talon into the socket of his eye…

He gathered his fear into his throat with a slow, steady breath, forced it into a tight ball, and swallowed it down. He forced his breathing quiet and even. His heart slowed in his chest, and the claw retracted, if it was ever truly there. The facade of peaceful sleep slowed his racing heart a bit. He reminded himself that, even if he didn't believe it, his mother was right. The fear was all in his head.

It was just as he was on the brink of sleep that the whisper came from next to him.

"Elisha."

He startled awake, a little cry of fear tumbling from his throat. In the gloom, he could make out a familiar shape next to his bed.

"For god's sakes, Gracie–"

"–*Don't* say that, Elisha–" his younger sister whispered.

"–You can't just show up in people's rooms all the time; it's creepy."

"But Elisha–"

He was embarrassed at the noise that had just tumbled from his mouth, and it made him less than charitable to whatever his sister wanted to say to him, so he put on a show of turning over in his bed and wrapping his blankets around him tight. "Go to bed, Grace."

She wasn't easily discouraged once she had decided to do something, which made her a particular kind of pest to older siblings. She crawled into bed and flopped all fifty pounds of herself on top of his cocoon body.

"*Stop* it, Grace. Go to sleep."

"I wanna show you something," she said, and began pushing her feet into the mattress to give her extra leverage to shove him with. "Get *up*, Eli, come *awn*." She drew out the last word long and slow, not quite a whine but teetering on the precipice of one.

"You're a pill," he said, which was a phrase his mom used when Grace threw a fit that he thought made him sound more mature than he felt. "You can show me in the morning if it's so important."

"But it's not going to *be* there in the morning," Gracie said insistently. She shoved him again with all the strength she could summon from her scrawny little-kid limbs.

"Leave me alone," Elisha snapped, and sat up so quickly his sister nearly tumbled off his bed. "You're so *annoying.*"

He thought she'd shove him again, which would mean he'd have to go downstairs and get his mother to make her leave, but instead Gracie sat back and looked at him with big-eyed remorse.

"Sorry," she said. "I didn't mean to be."

He felt a reluctant tug of guilt in his stomach and chewed the inside of his cheek. "It's fine," he said finally, and crossed his arms. "What do you wanna show me that can't wait?"

Her grin was missing four of her teeth in total, and in the grainy dark loomed like a jack-o-lantern face. "You know how Mom put those traps under the house? And, how you heard something running around down there?"

"Yeah?"

Their mother had suspected rats, or maybe a raccoon, opossum, or some other animal. It was an older house than the newly built apartment complex they used to live in. The man from the pest control company explained to Elisha while he was watching him work that sometimes animals moved into the cracks and crevices common in older houses. The kinds of nooks and crannies you didn't often think to check, unless you were a small, four-pawed thing searching for a warm spot to sleep. The man hadn't found anything, besides a few old mouse droppings, but he set up some traps and sprayed chemicals around the outside of the house.

When Gracie had heard tell of critters, she'd gotten excited at the prospect of a little mouse or even a rat or raccoon to rescue and keep as a pet. Secretly Elisha shared the sentiment, although he was old enough to know that racoons have rabies, so he was hoping for a cat instead.

She leaned in and whispered, "I left food out for it. Some crackers and an apple. And I checked it after, and it ate some."

"You shouldn't leave food out," he said. He didn't care so much if she did, but he felt obligated to chastise her, as the eldest child. "Anyway, it's probably bugs that're eating it."

"It's not bugs," she cried, loud enough that he had to shush her. She hated bugs. He was shocked she had the wherewithal to sneak off to the crawlspace in the first place, considering the number of cobwebs he'd seen down there. "It's *not*," she said, quieter. "I seen what was living inside."

"Saw," he said.

"Seen," she asserted confidently. "I seen what was inside, and I met it," she said, then she nodded to herself and leaned in conspiratorially. "There's an angel under the house, Elisha."

He decided to humor her. "An angel, huh? What does it look like?"

"I told you, it's an *angel*," she said, as though that explained it all. "It's very friendly, and it only comes out at night."

"Sure," he said. "Wings and all, right?"

"Lots of them," she said. She was shifting around on the bed, tangling and untangling the sheets in her legs.

"How many?" said he asked and yawned.

He was used to sharing a room before they moved to the old house and, although she was annoying sometimes, having her in his room again was comforting. Enough to remember that he was tired. He lay back, propping his head up on one hand so he could watch her.

"Umm," she said, and thought for a moment. "Two are its arms," she said, "And there's two it covers his face with. There's more too, but I forgot."

"The angel covers its face?"

"It's very shy, I think," she explained. "Its name is Pan-u-el"

"Mm." He made a little noise of agreement, but his eyelids were drooping. "Did you name him yourself?"

"No, it told me that Eee-nock was its name," she said.

"He talks?"

"Yeah. It told me that it came from our father."

Elisha's eyes opened at that, and he frowned. Gracie was too small to remember the divorce probably. She was just a baby at the time, and he was around her age when it was all settled. They didn't even keep photos of their father in the house. When he was younger, he used to ask questions about him all the time. . Whenever he asked, his mother would look nervous for a second before answering the question in a high and tense voice as simply as she could, still scared but acting like she wasn't. He had stopped asking, because now he was old enough to understand that he probably didn't want to know the real answers.

"Gracie," he said carefully, "Dad isn't… He isn't a good guy."

"Not *that* father," she said. "Father Martin."

Elisha sat up. "Who's Father Martin?"

"Our Father Martin Heaven," she explained. "We have another dad named Father Martin Heaven and he has a lot of angels."

"Well, I've never met him," he said, relieved. "He sounds like a deadbeat." He laid back on his pillow.

His sister was having none of it. She grabbed his arm. "Hey, don't go to sleep."

He yanked himself free. "Why not?"

"I wanna go see the angel with you," Gracie said.

Elisha thought about the long walk down the stairs, past the kitchen, and into the mudroom, where the tiny three-foot doorway into the crawlspace was. He thought about opening the crawlspace door and getting on his hands and knees, crawling into that creaking, writhing, cobwebbed blackness beyond.

"No," he said, and lay down. "Go to bed, Gracie."

She let out a wordless whine, then, high and keening. He ignored her for what felt like three minutes of her having a tantrum as quietly as she could.

"Fine," she said. "But I'm gonna go see the angel." She crossed her arms then stomped, which was silly. No one really did that except on TV.

"You can't go into the crawlspace by yourself," he said.

"Can too. I did *three* times so far."

"What if you get stuck in there?" he asked, remembering that the door had a lock only from the outside. "You know nighttime is when the spiders come out." Or worse. He thought about racoons and rabies again. "You'll get bit by a black widow and die."

"I won't," Gracie said, and stomped her foot again. "I went *three* times, and there were no spiders. You're just *scared.*"

His face got hot. "There's no angel down there," he said. "You're just telling tales." Another phrase he borrowed from his mom that she said a lot.

"There is. I seen it." Gracie was getting louder now and higher pitched as she worked herself up. "You won't get to see him because you're a weenie baby, but *I* did."

"Fine," he said, and whipped the sheets off his bed, swinging his legs over the side to get up. "Fine. I'll prove there's nothing there except spiders and bugs and maybe some rats."

Gracie seemed pleased by this and quieted down, much to his relief. She grabbed him by the arm and tugged him forward. "You'll like the angel," she said. "It's nice."

Elisha, who was still frightened and now annoyed his arm was being tugged on, was led forward with reluctance. The door to his bedroom was flung open, the yawning dark of the hallway beyond exposed. To distract himself, he made conversation.

"Where do you get all this angel stuff anyways?" he asked. "We don't go to church."

Instead of answering, she got distracted by the idea of church. "Do you think if I asked Mom, she'd let us go?"

"Who says I want to go to dumb church?" he said.

He'd been to a church once when he was small for a funeral, which was a stifling affair that involved wearing a suit and tie and sitting still for at least two hours without so much as a coloring book while listening to adults cry and talk about Jesus. He wasn't very keen on going back, even if there was less crying normally.

"Don't say that," Gracie cried.

He scoffed. She was acting like a brat today. Probably because she'd been getting up in the middle of the night all the time.

"Chase goes to church every Sunday, and he says it's nothing but some old guy talking then some songs and stuff."

Chase was Elisha's friend. Possibly his best friend. The last time they'd met up, Elisha had entertained the idea of asking him if they were best friends. When the moment came, though, he had felt too shy and decided not to. Chase's mother was the type who hung up crosses around the house, and whenever he mentioned going to church, he crinkled his nose like he was smelling something bad.

"I don't like Chase," Grace said.

They'd reached the end of the hallway where the stairwell started now. The hardwood of the stairs was cold underfoot compared to the carpet that lined the hall and bedrooms.

"Why not? He's nice to you."

It was true. Unlike his other friends, who either ignored Grace or mocked her behind her back for liking things like TV shows about ponies and sparkly dresses, Chase was very kind to her. It almost embarrassed Elisha sometimes how kind he was to her even when she interrupted them playing video games or trying out new bike tricks in the cul-de-sac. He even tried to include her sometimes, which was terrible because Elisha wanted to tell her to leave them be but didn't want to risk Chase thinking he was a horrible older brother. He chalked it up to Chase having no sisters at home, older or younger, so having Gracie around was a novelty.

"I just don't."

"Whatever." Elisha began descending the stairs.

He wished that Grace would ask him if she could hold his hand. He wanted the reassurance of a small, warm palm in his. But he was older, and a boy, so he couldn't bear the humiliation of asking, so he clutched the guard rail with his other hand instead.

She kept pace beside him, silently thinking as they descended. "I don't like the way you are around him," she said.

"Who, Chase?" Elisha asked. A nervous knot began to form in his chest. "How do I act around him?"

She didn't answer right away, and he wracked his brain trying to figure out what she meant. He acted the same way with Chase that he did with all the other kids at school. If there was any difference, it was because of Chase, not because of Elisha. Chase was different from his other friends. Elisha couldn't tell what it was exactly. Maybe it was because all the other kids at school had known that since they were in middle school, the cool thing to do was to be aloof and sarcastic, and Chase was the kind of boy who still thought light-up shoes were cool. Elisha thought that too and was secretly happy to see someone who didn't want to pretend they weren't just because they were almost teenagers. Maybe it was because Chase was kind, not just to Grace, but to everyone. Maybe it was because he was the only one of his friends who could do a 180 bunny hop on his bike. Maybe it was because he was the only friend of his who had dark hair and freckles, or the way his eyelashes were so long that he looked a little pretty up-close sometimes.

"You're imagining stuff," he said, when Gracie failed to come up with an answer in time.

They had come to the second landing. Five more steps and they'd be downstairs. He started down the last stretch when there was a small tug on the sleeve of his shirt. When he turned to look back it was too dark to see her expression, but he didn't have to.

"It's okay," he said. "There's nothing here at night that isn't there during the day," he repeated, and even though it didn't help when his mom said those same words to him, it helped a to repeat them to Gracie.

"I'm not scared of that," she said. "What if Mom dies? Or you die?"

He wasn't expecting that. "Why do you think we're going to die?"

Her voice quavered. "I don't want you to go to hell."

"Huh?" He was too taken aback to hold back his sudden confused sound. "Gracie, don't worry about it. I'm not going to hell."

She sniffled thickly. "Promise?"

He didn't go to church, but he was pretty sure that not going to hell wasn't something you could just promise. But he said anyway, "Promise."

"Okay," she said. "I'll have to ask the angel about it, though."

He took her hand in his, and together they traversed those final five steps. Now they had to be really quiet, since their mother slept in the bedroom downstairs. She was not a light sleeper, but it never hurt to be careful. Being in the dark now wasn't quite so bad, partially because the stairs and hallway were the darkest parts of the house, and partially because it felt like Elisha had spent so long submerged in it that by now he was used to it.

"Have you been talking to someone at school about church stuff?" he asked.

He pictured one of her classmates telling her that she was going to hell and contemplated the morality of hitting a six-year-old. He'd never beaten up anyone and was conflicted about the idea of hitting a first grader, but he was pretty sure he was supposed to beat up any kid that said that sort of thing to his sister.

"No, just the angel," she said. "And only a little bit. It told me that I wouldn't go to hell."

"Oh," he said. "Okay."

They crept past the kitchen, into the living room, and the hallway just off the mudroom. The moonlight illuminated the shapes of the furniture, outlining them in fine, pale white. He thought of ghosts and tried to put the idea from his mind, instead, imagining them as sleeping silhouettes of some other, friendlier creatures. The mudroom was ahead, a small room that smelled like a cupboard and housed the washer and dryer. Tucked next to it was the tiny doorway that led into the crawlspace, installed sometime in the past by the builders of the house for a purpose that escaped him. Why anyone would want to get into that humid, cobwebby, cramped space was beyond him. He imagined a boy who'd lived in the house previously, who was banished and locked in the crawlspace when he was bad by his cruel parents, like something out of one of his books.

"Wait," Gracie said, and dropped his hand.

"What is it?" Elisha asked, but she shushed him. He waited expectantly. "Is there–"

And then he heard it. A shuffling sound, low and quiet. A whisper of something just behind the walls, maybe, or under the floor. It was the sound of a satin sheet being pulled along a rough board, or the sound of grass sliding across the haunches of some slinking predator, or some other terrible thing that his mind could not imagine. He felt every hair on his body stand on end, his arms covered in gooseflesh. He felt a cold sweat begin on his palms.

The fear seemed to sharpen his vision in the dark. Gracie turned to him, and Her jack-o-lantern smile was glowing, the whites of her teeth shining in the pale moonlight. "I can hear it!" she whispered giddily.

"Gracie, I don't–" His protest was too quiet or too late. His sister was creeping toward the mudroom door. He followed, helplessly towed in her wake. The hallway through which the mudroom door could be accessed was much darker than the kitchen, darker still than the stairs, and his heart hammered in his chest as he submerged himself into its umbra. She grabbed the doorknob. The creaking, rusty hinges keened as the door swung open— a quiet wail that shuddered into something like a high, mocking laugh.

There was a slight breeze from inside the mudroom, a quirk in the air pressure of the house that sucked at the door and made it close from the inside even when you didn't want it to. This fact did little to assuage the cold chill of fear that Elisha felt when, at opening the door, a billow of hot, humid air hit his face. He felt something brush past his cheek and he batted at it instinctively, assuming it was a bug. The something settled on his hand, and he drew it to his face, pinching it between his fingers. It was a soft downy feather, pale and ghostly in his palm.

Grace was already inside the mudroom. She sat on the floor next to the crawlspace door. Elisha could barely make out her dark shape slouched on the linoleum. She fiddled with the latch, and then…

A pale white glimmer outlined the crawlspace door. He thought he'd imagined it the first time it happened, but…there it was again. A flicker, a distant gleam of white light. Then something behind the door moved. He heard it like a stone being rolled into place: a deep, heavy noise that tremored the ground beneath him. The edges of the crawlspace door suddenly glowed with blinding light. He wanted to shout at Grace, to tell her to lock the door again, the only remaining thing that could keep that cold light at bay. But Elisha was a pillar of sand, transfixed in horror where he stood, unable to move or speak and barely able to breathe.

Gracie's face was glowing in the corona of that inhuman light. She was grinning wide, wearing an expression of awe so deep it resembled fear, an emotion far too ancient for her small, smooth face. Slowly, she opened the door.

Elisha couldn't let himself see any more. He was a coward and would despise himself for years afterwards for it. He turned away from Gracie and the door and whatever was behind it and ran. If he had waited a second longer, seen the blinding glare of the door being opened a crack and the light drowning the room, suffocating it in that horrible cold glow, he might have seen the appendage that emerged from within to gently caress the awestruck face of his younger sister, face lit like the full moon on a clear light, paralyzed with sublime awe.

He wouldn't have any answers for his mother the next day, or the police. He would never be able to say for certain that he witnessed a pearly tear trace down the wide-eyed, innocent cheek of his sister as she moved toward the door, opening it wider, suffocating the room with the blinding white light.

After that night the light wouldn't return, nor the shuffling and movement beneath the floorboards. Nor would his sister ever return from the place where she was taken. He dreamed of her often. Even as the long years stretched his limbs and deepened his voice, she remained a child in these dreams, never growing into the young woman she was meant to become. He suffered her absence like a missing limb, a tightness in his heart and a heaviness in his bones.

He would live the rest of his mortal life in darkness. Only in his dreams would he witness true light, those blinding rays of heaven, and when he woke, he felt the pressure of the darkness weigh heavy and soft around him like a blanket, and he wept.

It Came Ashore
Robb White

Billy Fontaigne and his girl Jeanette O'Bannion had been dating since sophomore year in high school. Everyone who saw them walking around town holding hands thought they were such a cute couple. Their classmates voted them prom king and queen that year

Their families and friends were surprised when the couple went missing. When they were brought into the county morgue in a single body bag, the medical examiner had to pull Freddie, his assistant pathologist, off the motorcycle accident victim on New Bristol Road to help him sort out the organs and bones inside. Flesh hung in ribbons, and both sets of femurs showed signs of gnawing.

"You notice that smell, Freddie?"

"The deputy said they found the remains scattered on Highland Beach."

Fresh drowning victims arrived with an olfactory tinge of iodine on their skin. Those who'd been in the water a long time were internally bloated, swollen like the effects of trauma or septic poisoning victims with what used to be called 'third spacing' or the movement of intravenous fluid shifting from the blood stream; they carried a strong odor of decomposition, partially masked by the water absorbed in the body.

"No, something else," Doc said as he patrolled the edges of the steel table like a ferret closing in on a familiar prey.

The jumble of body parts on the table sent Deputy Carruthers reeling backward in disgust when the chief pathologist placed them out in view one at a time like fragile valuables. He'd controlled his nausea in front of the other deputies and volunteer officers well enough up to that point. Seeing them lying in a helter-skelter display sent a stream of vomit out before he could clamp a hand over his mouth.

"God damn it, Carl," Doc Peters roared. "Get out of here if you're going to do that."

Deputy Carl was only too happy to leave. He wiped vomit from his lips and headed for the ambulance dock out back rather than risk passing anyone upstairs who might know him.

Ever since Fred Hastings went from med school to the M.E.'s Office, he insisted on the formality of being called 'Dr. Hastings' by nurses and interns working in the hospital. Doc Peters never obliged him but tolerated his other eccentricities. Dr. Hastings was methodical in weighing organs and taking samples, but he relied too much on the flat overhand knot, the so-called 'European death knot,' for tying off the thread on the cadaver's thorax. Doc had scolded him that month for leaving a 'bulge' in one corpse owing to the bags of organs packed inside the chest cavity. He lacked the acumen of a good pathologist who did more than collect data; Freddie was adequate when it came to putting the evidence together to deduce a cause of death, but for the more complex causes of death, he was lacking. For that, you needed imagination and young Hastings was just a numbers man.

"There," Doc said, sniffing, latex-gloved fingers grasping the edges of the table.

He bent so low only his head was visible above the table. He'd detected it before it was overwhelmed by the other smells. It intrigued him because Doc liked solving puzzles. The humdrum ordinariness of corpses rarely posed a challenge. Northtown wasn't more than a mid-sized, rust-belt burgh and very fortunate to have two pathologists. Its citizens took a greater-than-typical zeal for helping their fellow citizens shuffle off the mortal coil in sundry but banal ways with guns, knives, and automobiles. Alcohol and fentanyl were the champs who did the majority of self-inflicted killing.

"Something there, just sitting on top of that normal decomp smell. Come here, Freddie. Take a whiff."

Doc moved out of the way to let his assistant duplicate his position at the table.

"Bend, damn it," Doc ordered.

"No, sir," Hastings replied, straightening. "It smells like rotten meat left out in the sun. That's all I'm getting."

The deputy told them all the remains were confined to a fifty-yard radius of Standing Rock, the famous landmark of Highland Beach where generations of swimmers standing on the rock offshore for photographs. They appeared to be walking on water in a depth that reached only to the ankles, a result of some glacier millennia ago pushing boulders across the Great Lakes Basin in what would become the shallowest of the five Great Lakes, Erie. The single boulder was surrounded by open water. Last year, one enterprising citizen robed himself like Jesus of Nazarene and posed for a photo that went viral to the chagrin of local church leaders.

Two hours spent sorting through and assembling the ghastly debris on two steel tables resulted in neither occupant of a table looking remotely human, much less male or female, especially with missing heads.

Doc liked a drink or two after work and headed for Shenanigan's Bar opposite the hospital. Cops loved gossip but not when outsiders invaded their territory. Doc had a grudging membership in that elite group by dint of his intimate association with the same people the police dealt with, the only significant difference being he met them when they were deceased.

Lieutenant 'Babe' Morehouse was holding court when Doc walked into the dark bar late that afternoon.

Morehouse spotted Doc at once and beckoned him over. "So, what was that asshole casserole on the beach all about?"

"You're supposed to be the cop, not me," Doc said. "What's your theory so far?"

"They went joyriding on the lake in somebody's boat; got caught in that big storm last Tuesday. Engine stalled. Got knocked overboard by waves, drowned, and got chewed up in a passing lake boat propeller's wake." Morehouse slapped his hands together in satisfaction.

"And the teeth marks, Sherlock Holmes?" Doc asked.

"Hell's-bells, Doc. Fish did the rest, nibbling at the bodies while they drifted to shore."

"Can't be, and you know it," Doc said. "Not the way a propeller shaft rotates in the water. I'd have spotted the regular cut and slash marks. The evidence says chewing, tooth marks."

"Without the heads, how do you know for sure?" Morehouse still wasn't convinced. He liked playing devil's advocate to the pathologist; it was a game they both enjoyed from their different professional angles.

"Because the atlas was intact, and the cervical spine showed grooves like tooth marks," Doc said. He wondered if the cop he'd known for so many years had lost his edge. Morehouse wanted to close cases rather than investigate.

"The what?"

"The ring-shaped bone at the base of your neck. Called the atlas for the Greek god who—"

"Held up the world," Morehouse said. "Yeah, I went to college, too, Doc. I wait upon your preliminary report with bated breath."

"When I write it up, you'll see 'tooth marks' all over it," Doc said.

"Christ, Doc," Morehouse huffed. "There's nothing in the lake bigger than a muskellunge or walleye with teeth capable of doing that damage. You're thinking sharks, and that's Florida, not Lake Erie."

"I go where the facts take me," Doc insisted and raised two fingers to Ruby, the bartender, signaling his boilermaker. "Thought they trained you cops to do the same."

"No more," Morehouse deadpanned. "They make us watch cop shows on TV."

After a pause, Doc asked him, "What else did you find?"

"You mean, like footprints leading to a homicidal maniac? Nothing. The usual crap that washes up after a big storm. Seaweed, beach whistles…"—cop slang for the tampons women flushed down the toilet and washed up on the beach— "driftwood, garbage. Somebody's skiff floated in from Redbrook marina."

The missing couple was rumored to have eloped. Their parents had nothing to contribute to the mystery of their absent children and were still in shock. But the cops reported no missing small craft from the marinas that could have explained how the couple wound up far out in the lake, enough to arrive onshore with that kind of damage in so short a time.

It bothered Doc all night and the next day. He put his assistant in charge in his tiny office and headed out.

"Where shall I say you've gone, sir?" Freddie asked.

"Tell them I've gone fishing."

Highland Beach was a popular spot in Doc Peters's youth for teenagers to drink or throw down a blanket and neck with your girlfriend. Swim out to Flat Rock and take a photo of yourself posing in a Tae Kwon Do *kata* or, like the anonymous joker on *Facebook*, who took a recent selfie dressed up like Jason Vorhees in a hockey mask while stabbing the air with a butcher knife. Cops wanted to talk to him after Fontaigne's and O'Bannion's remains washed up. He pleaded his innocence with Det. Morehouse by showing him older selfies when he was Christ at the Last Supper, Billy the Kid, and Batman, too. The erosion by decades of wind and water had altered the shoreline so that a spit of beach was all that remained. In recent years, it proved deadly. Intense wave action from southwesterly winds that funneled down from Canada created rip currents in rough weather. In Doc's tenure, five bodies had wound up on his tables, including two fishermen last year from a capsized bass boat.

He followed the shoreline, savoring the iodine tang in the air. Morehouse was right. The beach was strewn with washed-up debris, especially clumps of seaweed like green Halloween witch hair sold in shops. The only clear space was a twenty-foot border up against the sandstone cliffs that shielded Highland Beach. That storm would've washed evidence of animal tracks or bear paws, if you bought into Freddie's hare-brained theory of a massive black bear wandering into the harbor. Doc snorted in contempt at the mental image of a bear lumbering past storefront windows on Bridge Street to get past the docks to the breakwall and then swim out to Highland Beach

So far, the algae blooms hadn't reached the eastern end of the lake. Bad enough that thousands of tiny silver shad littered the shoreline in a die-off and filled the air with the stench of their rot. He walked the beach, dodging the small waves before they drenched his shoes, inspecting the lake wrack for evidence of—something. Dead carp and sheepshead, major casualties after storms, were being picked apart into morsels by swarming flocks of gulls that blew up in a white whirlwind when he approached. They screeched their protest at his every step; a few brave ones barely exerting themselves to scatter at his approach only to return to the feast.

So far, Morehouse's theory held sway in the Northtown *Herald-Tribune* of drowning victims ravaged by massive propeller blades from a thousand-foot lakeboat with an engine thrust of 8,000 horsepower, which would make mincemeat of anything not solid steel in the water.

A chunk of plywood floated just out of reach. It appeared too new to have been in the water long. He waded out to fetch it, ignoring his soaked shoes and pantlegs. Just ordinary plywood.

Turning it over, a symbol of a fancy bird and the faded letters of a word or phrase were almost washed away by the surf: *a me ri ka. America? Made in America?*

Maybe a company that made wood products and had the American eagle for a logo? He thought of tossing it behind him onto the shore but changed his mind. What was its relationship to two corpses brought in as though they'd been put through a woodchipper? He sought answers to a crime scene that was literally fluid. Killers dumped bodies in water to remove traces of evidence. Despite the heat of the late-august day, he realized his mind had already jumped ahead: he was thinking 'killer,' not accident

"No propeller wash did this, Detective, you numbskull," he said aloud, alone on the empty beach except for the squawking gulls. "No school of walleye, either. I've seen the marks."

Northtown had a killer with teeth big enough to scrape bone and snap a humerus like a diner picking at a chicken wing at KFC.

***

"Mighta been a big old black bear, Doc," Freddie said again, the second time since he'd arrived that morning whistling Barry Manilow's *'Copacabana'* offkey as usual and setting his Styrofoam coffee in the same spot for the last five years.

"The fallacy of repetition, my boy," Doc said, half-listening.

He adjusted the focus on his microscope. Like everyone else in Northtown bristling with theories of the couple's demise, Freddie championed his pet theory of a rogue bear surprising the young couple during a midnight walk along the beach.

Doc explained in the silence: "Repeating something doesn't make it true."

He examined the saliva sample from the rape kit. Nothing like DNA from buccal epithelial cells—better than blood for DNA testing. The rapist was a biter, and he sealed his doom with the rape kit brought over that morning. Many women shower away the attacker's repugnant filth as soon as possible.

Freddie wasn't done opining: "It could have wandered in from the Allegheny Mountains over to PA, you know, and decided to attack two kids walking along the beach."

"I'll give you credit," Doc sighed. "Your theory makes as much sense as Morehouse's propeller shaft."

Nothing galled Doc Peters more than writing the words *Undetermined Death* for the cause on his reports.

"I love white blood cells," he crooned, peering through the lens again. "Nothing like 'em for high purity and high molecular weight."

He'd grudgingly signed off on the release forms for the remains of the two teenagers that morning, each headed to a separate final disposition—namely, the chosen mortuary for the memorials. He refused to call the deaths 'accidental' and had zero evidence of homicide. What went into the closed caskets wouldn't take up a fraction of the room. Black bear sightings around the county were a dime a dozen in summer, but a bear attack would have left some evidence of its presence on the beach.

Although there'd not been a fatal bear attack in decades, it wasn't out of the realm of the possible. These apex predators wandered in from Pennsylvania during mating season; they normally confined their predation to house pets, mainly small dogs. Coyotes, on the other hand, were making a comeback in the county, but so far, no joggers reported hearing their chorus of yips or being harassed along the more isolated trails.

No predator existed for a thousand miles that could have done it other than a bear, people reasoned in chat rooms and online discussions. For one big enough to maul two adult-sized human beings—townsfolk reasoned—it had to be a Kodiak Island, grizzly sized monster.

But the theory-of-the-week most favored on *Facebook* impugned the deaths to a serial killer who drugged and abducted the couple, then dismembered them in his garage with a Stryker saw like Doc's bone saw. The killer scattered their remains on isolated Highland Beach for the gulls and rodents to devour. Freddie scoffed at the level of depravity that would take until Doc quoted Sherlock Holmes to him: "'The lowest and vilest alleys in London do not present a more dreadful record of sin than does the smiling and beautiful countryside.'"

Police Beat in the *Trib* reported frequent break-ins of garages and summer cottages near the lake and around the harbor area by amateur sleuths looking for a spectacular bloody crime scene. One disturbed individual was apprehended by police in a couple's yard where he'd fallen from their second-story roof trying to break in. He told cops he 'knew' the couple was guilty because they played Mozart's *Requiem* at all hours of the night.

Doc mused as he headed east along the shoreline toward the public beach. He carried the shard of wood along, slapping his leg in time with the waves rolling up to his soaked shoes. His best thoughts often came on these solitary walks. Sounds of distant beachgoers traveled on the air to reach him; a muted chord of excitement at play in the warm fresh water of Lake Erie. A thrill he'd enjoyed every summer in his youth. People appeared through the haze of a summer heat mirage as he got closer to the public beach. Semi-nude bodies prone in the corpse-like stillness of sun worshipers everywhere; families on blankets, in the water at varying depths; others farther out, just bobbing heads on the surface. Closer to shore, children splashed, with flailing limbs, threw water at one another, and screamed joy.

The epiphany was slow in coming. When it came, Doc was convinced he *knew* who the killer was. It was another axiom of the famous fictional detective that came abruptly to mind after that knowledge: "'When you have eliminated the impossible, whatever remains, *however improbable*, must be the truth'…"

Not a psycho killer, not a bear—then what? The pungent smell when he opened the body bag, like ammonia. The chemical symbol NH$_3$ popped into his head. *The board—*

"This board's a clue," he said aloud, well out of earshot from the bathers on the crowded beach.

"The language, it's Indonesian," he said, stopping in mid-stride. "It has to be."

He wasn't willing to express his theory aloud to anyone without evidence—and there had to be evidence if he was right about the killer.

Where to look? Between the narrowed peninsula of Highland Beach and the football-field-wide public beach, there were sand dunes dotted with salt meadow cordgrass and sea oats. The nearest houses at the top of the hill overlooking the lake wouldn't see it, nor would that multitude of happy beachgoers have any idea what could be lurking beyond the dunes in the thick tangle of undergrowth and vegetation that screened off the houses.

For the first time, a *frisson* of fear rippled up his spine. But he had to know. He walked into the dunes, all senses on alert. His ignorance of things Indonesian extended beyond the language, but the questions flooding his mind for answers were simple: How fast is it? Can it smell me coming? Can I outrun it in sand? He had a sickening image of a giant tongue flicking the air and an open mouth with bacteria worse than any sewer. A nick from one tooth could cause a fatal sepsis. He imagined a limb swollen to balloon-like proportions and banished the onset of icy panic.

Approaching the tree line—a ragged canopy of wind-stunted trees that rimmed the area between the concession stand and the boardwalk leading to the shoreline, Doc saw parents, toddlers on nearby blankets. He coldly assessed whether the beast would be sated with what it had consumed of the teenagers. If it lay quiescent and camouflaged among that dense shrubbery, would it waken with a ravening hunger for more fresh meat?

He didn't consider himself a coward, but he thought it the better part of valor just then to make a strategic retreat. Retracing his steps back toward the beach, he was surrounded by the lake breeze carrying varying scents of oiled flesh, citrusy perfume, fried foods from the concession stand's fryers, and something else that pinged his reptile brain: skin warmed to a level just under the register of a burn. That smell would magnetize a predator and send the salivary glands into overdrive. Not just the bacteria-laden drool pouring from its mouth, but the venom glands would release a toxin to send a bitten prey into shock and lower blood pressure. Even though he wasn't one of those TV medical examiners who put a half-eaten sandwich on the cadaver they were cutting up, he had long ago developed the iron-clad stomach of a veteran pathologist. For the first time since med school when his instructor took the class to see its first autopsy, he had that twinge in the belly when the chest bone was cracked open with rib shears and the reeking effluvia engulfed the students in a miasma of decay.

"Faster, go faster," he commanded himself as he scissor-walked to the parking lot and headed uphill to Walnut Boulevard.

His car was a mile away opposite Highland Beach. It wasn't fear that gave his legs speed but the thought of those people behind on the beach. If he was right, and he was convinced by now that he was, they were in danger from the couple's killer. And not one of them, regardless of age or size or athletic ability, could outrun the monster hiding behind the sand dunes.

***

Google Search and *Translator* confirmed his hunches. The bird wasn't an eagle or a logo; it was the symbol of the republic of Indonesia called a Garuda Pancasila—a mythical eagle-like bird that carried a shield and a scroll in its talons.

He played around with the words in Scrabble fashion for a couple hours until he found the right combination of letters to mean something in Indonesian; It raised the hackles on his neck. *Jangan Memberi Makan* translated to three words, not one: 'Do Not Feed.'

And what was not to be fed in that wooden crate that fell overboard in a storm? Something that should never have been removed from one of its islands in the Indonesian archipelago where the monitor lizards were protected under the aegis of a UNESCO World Heritage Site. He learned there were four islands as homes for the massive lizard that had undoubtedly been captured illegally and brought so far from its habitat. Of them all, Komodo, Rinca, Flores, and Gili Motang, only Komodo Island had the National Park preserved for the huge monitor lizards. But Rinca was infested with them and had the largest and most dangerous of these apex predators able to capture small deer and wild boar. They've added human beings to their menu, especially idiotic tourists and nature enthusiasts too eager for close-ups with the formidable beasts.

The more he learned, the queasier his stomach turned. They stalk prey with patience, using their coloring and the jungle for camouflage, able to smell prey from miles distant. Their muscular bulk enables them to scurry with deadly speed when they go for the kill at twelve miles-per-hour. They bite with a force of 600 psi. Trying to outrun a three-hundred-pound, aggressive male known to throw up the foul contents of their stomach to increase speed was easy—if you happen to be named Usain Bolt or Tyreek Hill. For the rest of humanity, running at six miles per hour is average; only running for your life with an adrenalin jolt could match the Komodo's speed, even though you'd never outlast its patience if it tracked you.

He stopped reading about the ancient, vicious creature when he came to the part that said they were known to be cannibals, feasting on their own kind. The final sentence said males would mate with a dead female if 'her body was still warm.'

"Jesus Christ, save us," he whispered. The survival instincts of these killers were like nothing ever seen on the planet since the age of dinosaurs

He called Shelley Duplessis at the *Trib*, the crime-beat reporter, and told her his theory.

"We have to get the word out," he said, "even if my theory is wrong. I know it sounds crazy but—"

"Doc, you need to lay off the boilermakers at Shenanigan's. I switched to dirty martinis and cut my hangovers in half, man."

He thought about calling Morehouse next, but the cop's wicked sense of humor would make him the butt of barroom jokes for years if he were wrong. *But I'm not wrong, am I?*

He couldn't sleep that night and tossed in his rumpled bed until dawn. In his final dream, he was chased along the beach by one of these giant lizards, its slavering mouth and razor teeth inches from his fleeing feet. *And what happens if it goes rampaging on a crowded beach? Who's responsible then?*

He called the precinct and was patched through to Morehouse at a location in the harbor. A young woman on a three-day meth binge had wandered off into the brushy hillside above Bridge Street and was bawling for help;

two Good Samaritans went to her aid, but she refused to come out and claimed she was caught in pricker bushes. Morehouse was supervising his crew of officers trying to cajole her out of there.

He listened to Doc's story in stoic silence while Doc ticked off his list of 'evidentiary items,' hoping to convince the detective with reasoning. When the call ended, owing to Morehouse's 'other emergency,' Doc was left unsatisfied and had the feeling he'd made a mistake.

He was right. Following up on his call, he heard giggling in the background when the lieutenant put him on speakerphone. Doc was the laughingstock of the precinct and found himself fielding calls from colleagues asking him if he was 'all right.' By shift's end, he had no doubt his call to the lieutenant had proved to be a four-star, revolving disaster. Dropping in to Shenanigan's only confirmed the worst: every cop at the bar turned around on his or her bar stool to salute him with hoots of derision or a wide grin and a whiskey tumbler raised in a mocking toast.

"Thanks a lot, Babe."

"Well, Doc, what did you expect?" The cop's grin in the stained bar mirror was ear to ear.

Doc signaled for his customary drink, tossed it down his throat, and winced at his reflection in the mirror as the scorching liquid burned its way down his esophagus. He got off his stool and bolted for the exit.

"Hey, where you off to?"

"I'll get you your damn proof," Doc threw at the cop over his shoulder.

He exited the bar with catcalls and jeers echoing behind him.

Back home, he called the Coast Guard in Cleveland and was told that dozens of small craft had foundered during the storm on that Tuesday. No saltwater or Great Lakes freighters had called in emergencies—with one exception: the *SS Ampana* had come through the St. Lawrence Seaway the Sunday prior. Its cargo manifest listed a bizarre assortment of dry goods ranging from crude palm oil and rubber to shoes, copra, and electronics. They notified the Coast Guard on the emergency channel during the storm to report 'a port-side listing' when the starboard ballast tank pumps failed. The captain later claimed that power had been restored, and the ship was proceeding to its scheduled berth in Toledo.

"No live cargo aboard? No animals?"

"That would be a violation," the Coast Guard officer said.

"I assume the ship was inspected before it left port?"

"It's international law," the officer said.

"Where was the distress call made?"

"The lat and long make it, oh say, five nautical miles off Northtown harbor," the Coast Guard officer told him.

"Where was the ship registered?"

"Jakarta."

How difficult would it be for a corrupt ship's captain to take a bribe from someone asking to put a wooden crate aboard, no questions asked? Some rich eccentric who collected specimens for their rarity. *YouTube* was full of people with bizarre, dangerous, and exotic pets. Doc had no choice and no one to ask for assistance. He thought of reaching out to Fred Hastings at home but pulling rank on a subordinate was contemptible.

Outfitting himself in the backcountry hiking gear and snake boots mothballed in the back of the closet decades ago gave Doc a dose of desperately needed courage on top of the sour residue of his single boilermaker still roiling in his guts. He grabbed his titanium trail flashlight from the top shelf and headed for the garage. Police ended their patrol of the beach area at the roundabout next to the concession stand a hundred yards from the shore.

He'd last gone offroad in a Jeep three Jeeps ago. Driving over the steel swing gate at the beach entrance meant to keep teenagers out at night was no difficult task for the Wrangler. He bypassed the parking lot and drove over the grass near the concession stand to the border where private beaches intersected the scrub and had been left undeveloped since the town's founding. The large houses above had a grand view of Lake Erie and weren't entitled to the land below their sloping, manicured lawns.

He parked, got out, and tested his flashlight away from the view of the lit windows high above. The local *Facebook* watchdogs and gossips posted dozens of comments about homeless men and women lurking in that area after dark. Drug addicts were spotted and reported to police like rare bird sightings. He hoped none were there. It was hard enough convincing rational people of his big-lizard-on-the-loose theory without having to explain to junkies why he was invading their privacy on a dark night with a new moon and few constellations for lighting. The sodium arc lights of the parking lot took on an orange haze in the muggy air. He was already sweating.

Where to enter the brush? It all looked the same. A thick dark curtain alive with insects and the small scurrying noises of rodents.

He wrapped a bandanna around his mouth to reduce the lashings from branches and pricker bushes, Gritting his teeth, he went into the underbrush and tried his best to reduce the noise of his slow advance. Prickers ensnared him, wrapped themselves around his thighs and knocked him off balance. Twice he fell. The ground was sandy but nothing like the difficult footing in the dunes. When his boot was stuck in a tangle of brush, he shivered at the thought of being pinned here. He'd crawl naked to get out if he had to. His progress was slow, and the perspiration dripping from his face and forehead made his eyes sting from the salt. A partial clearing at last where his flashlight revealed a space where windblown sand from the beach had reduced the vegetation to only the hardiest of plants able to survive. He played his light over the ground, searching for evidence. Nothing. Nothing smaller than a backhoe would leave signs in this jumble of sparse foliage.

His nostrils were filled with a pungent reek. As he swept the light from side to side, it nicked the corner of something—a clump of cone-shaped matter the size of a small anthill. He walked toward it and focused his beam on it. White flecks sparkled in the glare. Bone. Bone fragments. It was animal dung with an excruciating stench. He'd smelled worse on his table when cops brought him a hoarder's corpse rotting for weeks in his filthy house in a hot summer. The man saved his excrement in the single-use bags stores handed out.

Not just bone. Pieces of other things, what appeared to be the band of a cheap watch. Poking at the pile with a stick, he turned up more items—a belt buckle, a finger with the class ring from Harbor High School dated twenty years ago, a loop of human entrails, hair with a ragged attachment of scalp, and more bits of unidentifiable plastic and fabric. He replaced his leather gloves with his latex, careful to keep from contaminating the evidence bag he took from his shirt pocket and placed the finger with the ring in it. He used another bag to gather a sample of the dung.

The reek in his nostrils took a sharper edge—that same ammoniac smell he'd detected from the couple's body bag. *The scent of the dragon—*

He flew in the direction he'd come, running at

breakneck speed into the thick underbrush, mindless of the facial lashings from twigs. Whenever he was stuck in pricker bushes, he yanked himself free with heroic thrusts of his body, twisting himself to get loose. The monster on his heels was all the energizer he needed. At last, stumbling free onto the grassland by the concession stand, he gulped air into his lungs and sobbed hysterically.

I have the proof now, you bastards—

The wings fear lent to his feet was subsiding into a sickening nausea that caused him to lean over and heave up a stream of yellow bile. Heart thumping, locked in tunnel vision, he wanted to get out of there as fast as possible. Images of the dragon pounding its way through the path he'd taken were all he needed to recover and climb inside the safety of his vehicle. He drove drunkenly from side to side all the way home. His knees buckled in his driveway, and he collapsed on the asphalt, gasping for more air.

Inside his house, he stripped off his sweaty clothing and showered for a long time. Hot needles billowed the air with a soothing fog. Switching to an icy spray to revive himself mentally for the tasks ahead, he put on his bathrobe and headed for his clothing strewn around the foyer. His biggest options were to drive to the lab for tests or call the police to report his discovery.

His pants and shirt were wet and ripped in a dozen places. The bags were missing. He hadn't noticed in his terror. The thought of going back there to find it made him sick with fear.

He poured himself a tumbler of Scotch and collapsed on his sofa. He'd retrieve it in the morning.

"I'll take them right to Morehouse and shove both bags in his face," he said to his dark living room.

***

There were dozens of theories about the disappearance of Doc Peters. Lt. Morehouse even asked the FBI for assistance. His Jeep was found in the parking lot at Walnut Beach two days after he failed to show up at the hospital. Assistant pathologist Frederick Hastings was often quoted in the series of articles done by the *Herald-Tribune* about his lack of knowledge of his supervisor's abrupt absence.

Not known to buy a round, the young pathologist was often seen in Shenanigan's holding court and buying drinks for anyone who'd listen to his theory of Doc's disappearance. His 'wild bear' theory had shapeshifted into a popular serial-killer-on-the-loose theory subscribed to on and offline by many people in town. Disparaging his boss didn't help Hastings when he was briefly considered 'a person of interest' by Det. Morehouse, according to a Cleveland *Plain Dealer* piece after the subsequent disappearances of others in Northtown

Freddie, however, reveled in the media attention. When he was promoted to Interim Chief Medical Examiner, he organized a memorial service for Doc Peters. At the 'unofficial wake' later that night at Shenanigan's, no one mentioned Doc's wacky theory of a 'giant lizard' so as not to sully his memory.

Even the FBI took it seriously when a man out walking his dog near the breakwall didn't come home. He and his wife had 'marital issues,' according to the *Trib* article, and it was believed he simply took off for parts unknown. Being a heavy boozer lent credence to the theory.

As summer waned into fall, other cases of missing people and animals occurred. Northtown made the national news in a segment titled: "The Lakeport Town with the Big Curse."

The anchor narrating the segment took her viewers to the breakwall where the last person to go missing was a well-known fisherman. They found his fishing rod where he'd propped it in a crevice on the massive granite boulders forming the mile-long breakwall to the lighthouse at the harbor's entrance. She also interviewed a local birdwatcher who said he was looking from his hilltop backyard at the observation deck behind the breakwall where sightseers and hikers could observe the serene inlet's waterfowl activity. He saw a man flattened on the deck being dragged off kicking and screaming but didn't see who the culprit was, he said, because by the time he got back with his binoculars, everything seemed normal, the inlet waters serene as ever dotted with multitudes of lily pads. She didn't mention that the cops had investigated the man's claim and dismissed it owing to his infrequent stays in the hospital's fifth ward where mental patients were treated. One intoxicated boater claimed he saw 'something big' swimming offshore at dusk that didn't look like a man in the water.

Fall devolved into winter. Hikers along the breakwall trail reported seeing frozen carcasses of deer that had been field-dressed by a maniac, according to one hiker in the harbor's *Facebook* page. Bones of rabbits and groundhogs as well as Canada geese were found all over the one-hundred-thirty acres of wetlands by the breakwall. "Coyotes were back," the locals said.

Lt. Morehouse was glad when all the ruckus and rumors caused by the disappearances subsided. He felt he and his officers were personally blamed for not solving it. Taking a ride with one of his junior officers down to the beach one afternoon, he told the officer the city would stop plowing down there next week after the first squall of the season predicted for that night.

"Forecasters said this winter will be bad, lots of

below-zero temperatures," Jones, his officer, said.

Morehouse grunted a laugh.

"What is it, Lieutenant?"

"I was just thinking of old Doc Peters and his goofy notion of a serial killer who did those two kids back in summer. I wonder how his killer would handle the cold down there in February."

It didn't feel right to mention Doc's 'big lizard.'

The young officer seemed thoughtful, then gave the cruiser more gas to get up the steep hill leading to Walnut Beach.

"I used to work for the water company," he said after a while. "That network of pipes near the intake valve to the lake is a steel jungle. They have dozens of big old heat pipes for the wastewater treatment plant, so I suppose, in theory, it's possible a killer could find a cubbyhole in that maze to keep himself warm—say, you're a serial killer hiding out, I mean."

"You idiot," Morehouse grunted. "You sound just like Doc."

Crimson Ladies
Serena Daniels

Evelyn stood frozen, her eyes locked on the man sprawled across the bed, a thousand unspoken questions clawing at her throat.

"How long has he been like this?" she asked the doctor without turning her gaze away.

"He was transported here yesterday by a couple who he'd stopped to ask for help," the man's posh English accent informed her. "You can speak with a constable about the particulars." She only nodded.

"What is his condition exactly?"

The man, who worked with her mother, resembled a ghost, he was that pale.

"It is the strangest thing," the doctor admitted. "He's got all these tiny mosquito bites, but he doesn't have the other symptoms. Even more disturbing is that he's lost so much blood that he was on the threshold of hypovolemic shock. Had he not come in time...I wouldn't be the doctor that you'd be speaking with."

She frowned. While she was working towards having

"Dr." added to her name, it wasn't in the medical field. Still, from what she remembered from her father-who'd been a paramedic and often tossed around medical jargon whenever he'd talked about his shift-hypovolemic shock might as well be a death sentence if not treated right then and there.

"Despite his dire condition," she began, "was he able to say at least what caused those bites?"

When the doctor didn't respond, she faced him for the first time since arriving and was surprised to see a man of his calibre was biting his lip as if he was unsure if he should answer or not. After a moment, he inhaled before he answered.

"He was able to make a statement before he lapsed into his coma, however we put it down to being delirious from the blood loss."

"And what did he say?" Evelyn's tone was serious and hoped to convey she just wanted him to spit it out, no matter how ridiculous the answer was.

"He claimed that...he was attacked by butterflies."

Both of her eyebrows shot up "He said butterflies?"

"There's no mistaking what he said." The doctor replied firmly

"Just that it was butterflies?" She asked incredulously.

"Actually," the doctor seemed to be remembering. "He called them by a strange name, 'Crimson Ladies'. Does that mean anything to you?"

She didn't answer aloud, but the way she pressed her lips together as she frowned and nodded seemed to be enough for the doctor to not offer anything else.

"How are his chances of recovery?" she asked as she turned to the bed.

"We've managed to transfuse enough blood for him to recover, however, whether he will actually do so at all will be up to him at this point." The doctor informed her.

She nodded again as her thoughts turned gloomy. *'Which means that there's no chance, if there's any at all, of him waking up and talking to me anytime soon.'*

"And is there any way for me to speak with the constable who helped to bring him in?" She needed some kind of lead on what just the hell was going on.

"He mentioned that he was going to return to check on the patient in about..." A rustle of fabric made her assume that the doctor was checking his phone. "An hour from now."

"I'd like to speak to him, if possible," she answered the unsaid question.

"I'll be sure to inform him of such; you may wait here until then."

She barely got out a "thank you" before she headed to the chair beside the bed as the doctor left the room. She took a seat but didn't pull the chair closer; they didn't have that kind of relationship.

'Damn it, Dan, if you're here in this state, then what the fuck happened to Mom?'

***

Crimson Ladies. *Papilio sanguinarae nocturna.* That's what her mother had decided to call them, as mentioned a couple of letters ago.

Linda Bonds, a well-known and respected entomologist, had been called six months ago to a remote part of the English countryside. It was the definition of remote- one couldn't even get Wi-Fi there. Word had been floating through the entomology community that a never-before-seen species of butterfly had been making themselves known to visitors to the settlement.

At first, Mom hadn't been keen on travelling to a

place that was cold, wet, and rainy (never mind the fact that butterflies don't like those kinds of climates), being more at home in hot, and humid jungles in regards to her research. But that had changed when the entomologist, who had decided to study these unusual creatures, had vanished without a trace. And Mom being Mom, didn't listen to her daughter's reservations about throwing herself headlong into danger just to follow the temptation of solving such a mystery, only compromising by bringing along her two most promising grad students.

And one of them was lying in the hospital, seriously injured and not even a single hair to indicate where Mom and Jamie had gone.

'She should have listened to me.' Evelyn rubbed her forehead to stall the headache that was forming. *'And I don't have a clue as to where to start until the constable gets here.'* She leaned back in the chair as she struggled to not fall asleep. She'd gotten on the earliest flight that she could book. It was late at night, and the time difference was now kicking the crap out of her. She hadn't even checked herself into a hotel yet, and the couple of bags that she brought with her were sitting in the corner of the room by the door.

I'll just close my eyes for just a moment. She did so, not even being aware of when sleep took over her.

***

The door opening jolted her awake, and she managed to make herself presentable enough before she and a man in a constable's uniform noticed each other.

"Miss Black, I presume?" he asked.

She nodded. "Tell me what happened." She didn't care if she sounded rude, but she wanted to get straight to the point so she could be on her way to find a hotel. The constable seemed unruffled by her abruptness, possibly even used to it.

"Yesterday evening, a couple was driving by the bog that bordered," he heaved a sigh, "Bloodwing Hollow." He gave another sigh,

She could sympathize as she herself had rolled her eyes when she'd learned the name of the area that this new species would be found.

"By some small miracle, he was spotted crawling weakly along the ground and was brought here. By another miracle, despite his near-death state, he was able to utter where we could find your contact information."

"And what attacked him," she stated neutrally.

The constable winced.

'This guy wouldn't be good at Poker... Not very English...'

"Yes, but that's probably a delusion from his injuries," he replied.

At this point, given that this is a new species that we know next to nothing about, I'm not going to disregard anything that's being said, no matter how crazy.'

"If I may ask, how exactly are you related to Mr. Murphy?" It wasn't the question that annoyed her, it was the fact that she hadn't had the chance to make her request.

"He's one of my mother's graduate students," she replied. "He went along with my mother and another graduate student to Bloodwing Hollow."

He'd already taken out a notebook and was jotting the information, presumably because the situation didn't appear to be a simple matter anymore. "And what are their names?"

"The other student is Jamie Cross, and my mother is Dr. Linda Bonds; she's an Entomologist."

As soon as they both finished, the constable simply

paused with his pen poised and a close look at his expression told her that he was putting two and two together.

"So, she's here for those butterflies, is she?"

"Yes, she calls them the 'Crimson Ladies.' The doctor informed me that Dan claimed they're what attacked him."

"Yes, and now it's beginning to make a little more sense now that I've spoken to you. I assume the reason that he wished to have you contacted was because of your mother?"

"I would think so, both men know perfectly well that if something were to happen on any of mom's expeditions that I would be the first person that was to be notified before anyone else, even my mother's university colleagues," she replied firmly.

"And when was the last time that you spoke with your mother?"

"I received a letter from her was a fortnight ago, however, I wasn't concerned because I knew that the mail service would be slow with the area being so far from civilization and the lack of service also meant that texting would be impossible. It was only when I got the phone call notifying me of Dan's hospitalization that being concerned was an option.

"And if you're wondering," she added. "Yes, she became interested in going to Bloodwing Hollow after she'd heard of the disappearance of the previous entomologist who had made the same journey, against my wishes."

The constable was quiet for a moment before he stared into her eyes. "Miss Black," he began. "A search party was sent out after we'd been supplied by other witnesses who had met your mother and her students. I do regret to inform you that there has been no sign of either of them, and the villagers claim to know nothing of their whereabouts." His phrasing raised her hackles, and she took a gamble with her next words.

"I assume that is what the official report will say," she began carefully. "But I would like to hear what your opinion is on the matter, constable."

"The fact of the matter is," he began; "these villagers...aren't exactly in tune with the rest of the country, and I don't simply mean the lack of technology... They appear to cling to old ghost stories that we'd long stopped believing in. They're quite known around these parts for their odd superstition of never venturing out of their homes once the sun goes down, claiming that spirits of the dead would come after those who wandered outside.

"Now, I don't subscribe to those kinds of stories, but there have, in the past, been some strange occurrences that have yet to be explained. There is one report given by a traveller, who had spoken to an innkeeper that had been at the destination they'd ventured to after they'd left the village. It was the innkeeper who technically made the report as a precaution..."

"What happened?" Her voice was neutral but against her will, the hairs on the back of her neck were standing up, wondering what it could mean for her mother.

"The tourist had reported that they'd been unable to sleep, happened to look out of the window at the village inn, and witnessed what she thought was a group of teenagers sneaking along the main road. She couldn't hear what they were saying, but she assumed that they were deliberately breaking the curfew in a bout of teenage rebellion. Just as the group was going out of her visual range, she swore she saw some sort of red cloud swarm around them. Some of them managed to get out, but one of them was caught up, screaming in pain, but not a soul came out to aid them."

Upon hearing the colour red, Evelyn felt her insides turn into liquid as something tickled in the back of her mind regarding her mother's letters.

"She went back to her bed and stayed there without sleeping. At dawn, she rose and looked out the window again. She witnessed a group of villagers carrying what she could only assume was the body of the unfortunate soul from the night before. All she could really see was this human-sized brown blob. Anyway, she left that day and, from what I hear, has yet to return."

"Hmm, that's quite a story," she said as she tried to grasp onto it all. "Does the woman have a history of psychiatric problems?"

"That was the first thing we checked, and no she did not."

"Has anyone come forward with a possible natural explanation for what she witnessed?"

"We kept this quiet to avoid frightening people, but we made discrete inquiries to anyone who might have been able to give some kind of explanation. None of them have been able to give a sufficient answer."

Her next question was stupid, but if something has happened to her mom, she had to know. "Just where is Bloodwing Hollow located?"

***

And that was how Evelyn ended up being escorted by the constable, who she now knew was named Moss. In his vehicle, they headed towards what was clearly a dangerous place, despite how ridiculous the story sounded. Her instincts told her that it wasn't too late to head back. If it had just been Dan and Jamie, she admittedly wouldn't have bothered to come at all, but this was her mother...

After her question and Moss's promise to bring her there, despite the reservations that she knew he had without him saying so aloud, the ride to Bloodwing Hollow was a silent one. While she couldn't read what was in his mind, she could sort through the jumble that was hers. After hearing that story, she continuously turned over in her head what Mom had written to her about what she'd been able to observe whenever she'd been able to actually see the butterflies.

Now that she'd thought about it, the letters were almost cryptic to her, but she'd been unable to put her finger on why until now. It was the curfew, which meant that Mom and her students would have only been able to observe them from inside wherever it was they'd been staying. So her information was sparse, at least at first.

Mom's first letter only detailed three things about the Crimson Ladies that stuck out to both women: they weren't diurnal at all, despite their wings being varying shades of deep red. While butterflies are diurnal, only their moth relatives were nocturnal (save for some members in the *Saturniidae* family), the one exception being members of the *Hedylidae* family, which had long been mistaken for moth's because they also shared the moths' dull colors and hearing organs that most butterflies lack. So, the fact that there was a nocturnal butterfly, that didn't seem to be a moth, that possessed a different color of wings, was most certainly enough to warrant the attention of experts.

But that train of thought also led Evelyn to think back to the story if it was in fact true, then that possibly meant that the Crimson Ladies also possessed hearing organs, because it sounded like the swarm had almost seemed to have targeted the group of teenagers after hearing them talking, as they appeared to have come out of nowhere rather than hovering around until they'd attacked, which alone was also unusual. Which now led her to believe that her mother must have thought of this as well but didn't voice it for she hadn't captured a specimen for study at that time.

However, it was the third thing that her mother had mentioned that sent shivers up her spine. The Crimson Ladies looked, in Mom's expert opinion, to be larger than the typical butterflies, with a wingspan that reached almost a foot wide—a size that made it impossible to miss seeing them.

'Oh, fuck.' Nausea welled up in her. Ever since she was a kid, she'd had no trouble being around tiny and small insects, what terrified her were the bigger and sometimes venomous insects that her mother had kept in a special room in the house. The kind that always made Mom warn her daughter that she was never to venture inside without her.

It surprised even herself that she'd chosen to follow in her mother's footsteps and was studying entomology at her university. She definitely had plans to stick with tinier, safer insects for her area of expertise-like ants, even the Bullet ant, despite the fact that their bites stung like a motherfucker. That first letter alone had made her glad that she was only a student who wouldn't have the opportunity of discovering a new species the way her mom would. However, the second and final letter provided further description, the kind that made her wonder now exactly how Mom managed to gather it, besides her phone, since Wi-Fi wasn't needed for pictures, or her pair of binoculars. The only other possibility was that she had ventured outside—a thought that put Evelyn on edge, even though it made no sense at this point.

And that further description, which had only raised her eyebrows when she first read it, now only made her close to fearful. How her mother had described the wings being so many different shades of red—deep crimson, maroon, and blood-red—all formed into intricate patterns of marking that were dark and vein-like and imitated the design of lace.

She had also somehow managed to see their bodies, which were sharply contrasted against the vividness of their wings, slender, elongated and a hue that was almost black. The words Mom also used were 'slight translucence', 'ghostly' and 'ethereal'; the latter two she'd almost never heard from her lips.

But the creepiest description had to be their eyes: tiny, red, and glowing that were easy to spot in the dark, if a bit faint. Just imagining it unnerved her.

That being said, part of her was beginning to become convinced that her mother had in fact done the reckless thing and gone outside to study them closely, no doubt without the presence of her students. Yet, if that was the case, then why had she been allowed to live to be able to write that letter? It wasn't like it was written by an imposter. Mom had a distinct way of writing, and Evelyn would have known immediately if it had been written by someone else and certainly would have made her way down here faster than the speed of light if that had been the case.

And if she'd gone outside previously, what had gone wrong this time? Something catastrophic must have happened if Dan had stumbled away from the village and into the hospital with such life-threatening injurie. Also, what about Jamie? Her mom? Were they dead? Did they manage to get away to somewhere else?

She had no idea what to think anymore. Her body wanted to sleep, her energy was drained from everything, but she managed, from sheer will, to keep herself wide awake to be able to leave the vehicle with her luggage once she'd arrived at Bloodwing Hollow. Which was right now as she could see some ancient looking homes coming up ahead.

"I'll be fine, constable," she said and smiled at him after he'd offered to help her. "I won't be here that long."

***

Evelyn didn't think that it was a good idea to just storm into the village and demand answers. They would just clam up further than they likely already had. After Constable Moss had fully left her, she parked herself behind the largest building that she could see. She was acting as a lookout to make sure that she wasn't going to be caught; but mostly she was carefully observing the people for any kind of clues.

What surprised her is that the people (at least the adults) were talking freely about 'the one who escaped', and that caused her ears to perk up and strain to hear better. Her stomach dropped when she heard them talking about 'the dead one' and 'the one who disappeared'. For the first time since she'd received that message about Dan, tears threaten to spill.

'I have to explore further. I must find out whose body they're keeping. But where is it?' That was something the people were tight lipped about where they were storing the corpse. She couldn't help but direct her gaze up at the grey sky.

'It's hard to tell out what time it is.' She checked her phone, which had already switched over to the time difference. *'It looks like it's almost night... I shouldn't stay out in the open, but I don't have a choice...'*

Now, all she could do was wait until a black sky was above her.

***

True to the story, after the sun set, the village became deserted and that left her free and clear to look around, so long as none of the locals got cute like before. However, that also caused further nervousness as there was no one there to help her should things go badly as before, although she strongly suspected that no one would help any as before.

They didn't even bother with any kind of outdoor lighting. The lack of technology she'd expected, but there weren't even any torches, so she had to rely on her phone's flashlight, but the battery was already at half-empty. She was going to have to be as quick as she could when moving around. Luckily, each of the larger buildings that she checked out first weren't very closed off, and it was easy to see if there was anything unusual inside. The description of the 'brown blob' was at the forefront of her mind.

Her curiosity was only satiated when she'd crept inside one closed-off building. By its contents, she guessed it was some sort of storehouse. When she'd reached a back corner, she covered her mouth on a gasp.

A body was there, and it was apparent from this distance why that tourist had given such a bizarre description: it was desiccated.

'Fuck! Breathe, Evelyn, breathe.' She slowly inhaled and exhaled through her nose as she didn't trust herself not to scream if she opened her mouth. *'Just examine it as if it's a specimen.'* She wouldn't be able to stay sane otherwise.

The height was more in line with Jamie's than with her mother's, but that didn't necessarily mean much considering the lack of flesh and fluids. Their clothing was shredded, only scraps of cloth remained, whether it was from the butterflies themselves or some kind of temporary insanity that caused them to rip at their clothing for a reason only known to them was something that she didn't even try to figure out.

The long pants weren't much help, as they were the same type all three had worn the last time she saw them, but it was the green, buttoned sweater that told her this was Jamie. Part of her was sad, but another part of her felt that combination of guilt and relief that one feels when a missing loved one hasn't been identified as a corpse.

This meant that her mother was still out there, but was she alive? Or had the butterflies devoured her as they apparently had Jamie, and she just hadn't been found yet?

'What should I do now?' Her mental voice wondered in confusion. She carefully backed away from Jamie's remains and made for the door and carefully opened it.

But someone had been waiting for her...

"What are you doing?" An old man in front of her grabbed onto her wrist, causing her to emit a small squeak. "You shouldn't be out after dark."

"I know," she choked out, trying to sound braver than she was. "But I had to come here and find my mother and see who that body belonged to."

"An outsider?" He shoved his nose against hers as he gave her a closer look. "Your mother?" His face had already been angry, but it changed to be outright thunderous as he seemed to realize something. His grip became tighter, and she was sure it was going to leave a dark bruise.

"The witch?" he shouted as he dragged her from the storehouse. No matter how much she struggled, his grip strong for someone his age. "You would dare to come here?"

"Witch?" she asked in confusion as a spark of fear formed inside. "I have no idea what you're talking about."

"Do not pretend. That woman came here claiming to wish to study those witch ghosts, despite our warnings not to. She had us fooled until she was witnessed out at night and the crimson ghosts didn't harm her."

'Huh?' She slackened somewhat as she tried to make sense of his words. *'So, she went out at night to study them, but what is he even talking about?'*

"That's when we knew, she'd come here with dark intentions; after all, witches always recognize other witches. And she'd even brought a couple of sacrifices with her."

"What have you done with them?" She regained her strength to struggle some more. "I came here because one of her students is in the hospital close to death, and now I've discovered the other one in even worse condition. What have you done with my mother, you bastard?" She raised her free arm, balled her hand into a fist, and pounded against the arm holding onto her, somehow noting that he was taking her past what could be the village square and was heading for what she guessed were the woods her mother had described seeing them live.

"And what the hell do you mean by 'witch ghosts'? You're not making a bit of sense."

"Blasphemer," he shouted before he turned around and used his free hand to deliver a slap that stung and was loud enough that the whole village had to have heard it.

"And do not pretend that you are unaware of the witches of the past returning in a seemingly gentle creature, thanks to the devil. They take the lives of whom they please and leave those they wish to induct into their coven. Even after we take care of them, they still claim them."

'These people are fucking crazy.' "Is this some kind of sick joke? Everyone nowadays knows those witch hunts only caused the deaths of innocents."

"Silence, witch spawn." They had passed through the tree line, and there was a large post set up, with smaller sticks surrounding it, with burn marks on it.

"No," she whispered. Her adrenaline kicked in as her attempts to free herself became more frantic. "Mom..."

Something changed in the air. It started to almost smell like...blood. The man halted, and he raised his head up and around until he stopped to look in one direction. She followed his gaze. A red mist descended upon them.

Oh shit. Her mouth gaped. *I guess this is the end, but I should at least go out doing what Mom likely did too: observe what I can.* She focused past the mist on the large dark bodies the red haze was surrounding. Those intricate wings made a sort of soft, eerie whisper, like the rustling of silk.

Her heart pounded at how graceful they moved in a pattern that was almost synchronized, like they were dancing towards them. However, as they got closer, they dove with a speed and precision that could only be described as terrifying and predatory.

She willed herself to remain calm as their glowing red eyes came into view, she could feel the malice in their cold and penetrating gaze, as faint as it was unnerving. She barely noticed when the man threw her towards the swarm.

"If you are guilty, they will not harm you," he shouted as the swarm descended upon her

She wanted to close her eyes, but she stared them down. To her shock, the swarm danced around her form, allowing her to look closely at their wings.

The vein-like markings were strange; they mimicked the delicate design of lace, but there were outlines of women's faces in there, too. They threw themselves onto the man. When they were clearly devouring him, she was curious enough to walk up to where he stood and took a better look at how the butterflies were feeding.

'Interesting.' They possessed proboscis more like mosquitoes, and their bodies weren't plumping up despite the amount of blood they were draining. She continued to stare even after the swarm engulfed him when he lost his balance and fell to the ground.

She had no idea how long it took until the swarm lifted off him, but his corpse was as desiccated as Jamie's. She expected them to fly away, but they glided back to her in unison and hovered in front of her. She couldn't say what possessed her to do it, but she lifted a hand and reached towards them, palm up. The swarm parted, and one of the Ladies that had been at the back came forward and landed on her palm. She gazed at the wings and saw...

"Mom?" she asked carefully when she saw her mother's visage among the lacy patterning.

The butterfly lifted off her hand and settled on her nose for a moment before she flew away, the rest of the swarm following as they took off deeper into the woods.

'Wait,' she wanted to say, but the word lodged in her throat. She stood frozen until the mist they created had dissipated. As she walked back to the village, she wiped away her tears.

She had to hurry, not wanting to be around when the people found him. She had to get her stuff and leave; it would be a very long trek back to the town.

At least she had the time to think about what she was going to tell the constable and how she was going to be able to retrieve Jamie...

White Mantis
Rose Strickman

The praying mantis greeted Stephen with a wave of its hooked front legs.

Stephen stopped, looking at the insect. It looked back. Around them, the garden buzzed with insect chants and birdsong, flowers blooming violently, the forest a deep, shadowed wall at the end of the property. The sun beat down, summer-hot, flooding the world with golden light.

In this light, the mantis glowed.

He frowned at it. "You're white," he said to the insect. "A white mantis."

The pearly mantis cocked its head and waved its antennae. It was indeed pure white, from the tips of its antennae to the end of its abdomen. Its wings, under their covers, glowed a faint green. He marveled, having not supposed there were any white praying mantises in this region.

The mantis lashed out, spiny forelegs pouncing. In its grip, the beetle wriggled, its legs waving. The mantis began to eat, its white mouthparts tearing into the flesh, pale eyes fixed on Stephen.

"Gross." He scowled, turned away, heading back to the house, and left the mantis to its grisly feast.

***

The house, Glen Fae, was huge, old, and dark. The summer sunlight filtered through ancient stained-glass windows and danced in dust motes to land in yellow rectangles on the old, faded carpets. Most rooms had stone fireplaces, all cold and empty. Forbidding Victorian furniture loomed in dark-papered chambers. Stephen sighed, depression descending. He'd left this house as a young man and had never wanted to return.

The kitchen door opened, emitting his sister Corinne. "Stephen?"

He turned to her, catching sight of his face in a gilded, bleary mirror. He was a dark-haired, gray-eyed man in his early forties, face scored, shoulders hooked. "What is it?"

"Where were you?" Corinne, in contrast to her brother, was small and fair in a washed-out sort of way. She seemed far younger than him, though only a year separated them. "Dad was asking for you."

"Oh." He stood back with a sneer. "Dad."

"He's dying, Stephen," she said sharply. "It won't kill you to show some respect."

"He's been dying for *years*, Corinne. Living in this damn mausoleum turned him into a ghoul. Just like you."

Her mouth tightened. "Yes, well, at least I didn't waste thousands of dollars on a useless degree only to beg for more money to fund my empty pipe dreams of being an artist who was too good to get himself a job."

"No, you just stayed here like a loser, sleeping in your childhood bedroom—"

"Children."

They broke off. Stephen glanced guiltily up the stairs, where the shadowed figure of Mrs. Arden loomed. The housekeeper's glasses flashed with reprimand.

"Your noise will disturb Mr. Cameron," she said. "Come upstairs, Stephen. Your father has been asking for you."

Stephen might taunt Corinne, but he'd never had the nerve to disobey Mrs. Arden. Head down, hands in his pockets, he sloped up the stairs to join her on the landing. She led him the rest of the way upstairs, her every line radiating disapproval. Mrs. Arden had never liked him much, and his recent behavior had done little to change her opinion.

She opened the double doors to the master bedroom. "Stephen here to see you, Mr. Cameron," she said to the still figure in the bed, and herded Stephen in with one stern glance.

"Ah, Stephen." The sallow face turned to him with a saturnine smile. "Good of you to come."

"Hello, Dad." Stephen approached, feet heavy with resentment and reluctance, to sit in the chair next to his father's bed.

He viewed the wasted, yellowed face, half-buried in pillows, with disfavor. Marcus Cameron had once been a leader of the community, the heir to an old and respected name, handsome and imposing. Now he lay alone, abandoned by all save his children and his housekeeper. His flesh was caving in, his eyes bitter with the knowledge of his impending death.

"How are you feeling?" Stephen asked, then felt foolish. Marcus clearly wasn't doing well at all.

"I've been better," said Marcus with his old biting humor. "But the pain isn't so bad today." He shifted in his bed. "It won't be long now, son, before you must claim your inheritance."

Stephen came alert at this. "Inheritance?" His mind raced, thinking what he could do with the money his father left him. Better still when he sold Glen Fae.

"Yes." Marcus fixed him with a penetrating gaze. "As you know, ownership of Glen Fae Hall always goes to the oldest son."

"Yes, Dad." Stephen tried not to look too guilty, thinking about his plans for the old place.

"Four hundred years it's been in our family." Marcus glanced around the bedroom with far more affection than what he'd shown his son. "It was partially constructed with wood brought from Scotland, you know. Real Scottish oak, taken from the forests of the old country by our ancestor, Robert Cameron. This wood brought with it certain…properties. Certain obligations."

Stephen fought not to roll his eyes. "Yes, Dad." *More of this ancient heritage and family duty bullshit.*

Marcus chuckled, as though he heard Stephen's thoughts. "I know what you think of all that. But just because you don't believe in ancient obligations doesn't mean they don't exist." He poked a thin, papery hand out of the counterpane. "See that box?"

"Yeah." It was an ebony wood box, inlaid with mother-of-pearl, sitting on the bedside table.

"Open it."

Stephen took the box and opened the lid. His eyes widened. There, nestled in a bed of green velvet, lay the loveliest, most intricately detailed statuette he had ever seen. It was carved from half-translucent white jade, almost glowing with its own light in the dim room.

It depicted, in exquisite detail, a praying mantis.

It brought to mind the white mantis he'd seen in the garden, and he fought off a strange shiver. "It's beautiful, Dad." And it was an exceptional treasure even in a house of treasures.

"It's yours," Marcus whispered. "Consider it an advance on your inheritance."

"Really?" Stephen could barely take his focus from the statuette. "Thank you, Dad."

"Oh, you're welcome," murmured Marcus, eyes gleaming.

***

Stephen took the box to his room. It always irritated him that every time he came home, he was assigned the bedroom he'd inhabited as a child and teenager, as though all his life as an adult didn't count. But this time he gave his annoyance barely a thought. Sitting on the bed, he opened the box again.

The statuette gleamed, jade glowing with smooth light. He touched it with a gentle finger. The stone was hard and smooth, the detailing tiny and intricate.

Carefully, he lifted the statuette from its velvet bed. It had a satisfying weight in his hand. Out of its box, the craftsmanship was even more astonishing. It was elegant and perfect, so realistic he half-believed it would wriggle its legs or flap its wings.

He placed it on the bedside table, where it balanced perfectly on its gemstone legs. He marveled again at the incredible craftsmanship. Perhaps, if he couldn't sell the house, this might fetch a pretty penny…if he could bear to part with it.

The gong rang for dinner, and he hurried off, leaving the jade mantis waiting on the bedside table.

***

"So, Dad gave you the praying mantis statue?" asked

Corinne.

Stephen forked salad into his mouth. "How do you know about that?" They were eating in the kitchen, Mrs. Arden bustling around them.

"Mrs. Arden told me." Corinne exchanged a knowing smile with the housekeeper. "So. He gave you the praying mantis?"

"Yep." Stephen smirked at his sister. "I guess he wanted me to have some of my inheritance early. But don't worry, Corinne. I'm sure there'll be something for you, too."

She glared.

"You want to be careful of praying mantises," said Mrs. Arden. "I've seen them in the garden. Savage things." She sounded more admiring than censorious. "I saw a female eating her mate once. Just turned and chomped straight into his head, right in the middle of the act itself."

"Now *that's* how to treat men," murmured Corinne.

"How would you know?" sneered Stephen. "When's the last time you had a boyfriend?"

"Sooner than you've had a girlfriend. Didn't your last one break up by text?"

"You'd better hope you can get another boyfriend soon," he snapped. "Because this won't be your house for much longer."

He had the satisfaction of seeing both Corinne and Mrs. Arden shaken from their smug complacency, blinking and disconcerted. "What do you mean?" Corinne asked in quite a different tone.

"I mean that once Glen Fae becomes mine, I'm selling." He hadn't meant to reveal his plans so soon, but now he was reveling in their shock and anger. "You'll have to find somewhere else to live."

"You—you can't sell Glen Fae." Corinne was white-faced. "It's been in our family for four hundred years."

"Yeah, well, might be time for a change, huh?"

A strange sound invaded the kitchen, like an angry creak of wood, mixed with the buzzing of insect wings. Mrs. Arden took up a pinch of salt and hurried to the kitchen door.

"Knock it off," she snapped, casting the salt through the open door. The noise abruptly halted, leaving silence and darkness in its wake.

She closed the door and turned her glasses on him. "That, Stephen," she said, "was a very stupid thing to say. The Others heard you. And I'm guessing they're not happy."

"Oh, yeah, the *Others.*" He rolled his eyes. "The magic creatures living in the walls. I'm not five years old anymore, Mrs. Arden."

"More's the pity. You used to listen to me back then." Mrs. Arden shook her head. "You're messing with forces you don't understand, Stephen. You're betraying ancient bargains for childish reasons. And if you don't turn back, you're going to suffer for it."

"Right. Ancient bargains." He stood and put his plate in the sink. "I'm sorry, Mrs. Arden, but that's all bullshit. And once Glen Fae is mine, I can do what I want with it." He stalked out of the kitchen.

"Ah," Mrs. Arden murmured as the door swung closed behind him, "but what will Glen Fae want to do with you?"

***

Corinne and Mrs. Arden will just have to accept reality, Stephen thought as he prepared for bed. Mrs. Arden he could pension off easily enough, but Corinne might do something stupid, like bring a lawsuit against him. He smirked. Well, it probably wouldn't take long for his little sister to spill her stories about the Others in the walls, then the court would throw out her suit without discussion.

Yes, it would be good for Corinne to leave Glen Fae. He tried to quell his guilt as he settled into bed. She'd been here too long, refusing to grow up. Facing the outside world might mature her a little. He scrolled through his phone in the light of the bedside lamp, while outside the crickets started their nighttime songs to the accompaniment of frogs howling in the pond.

He read until his eyelids grew heavy. Reaching over to snap off the lamp, he noticed he'd forgotten to put the jade mantis away. It still gleamed on his bedside table. He'd have to pack it away tomorrow.

Darkness followed the dousing of the lamp, and he fell almost instantly asleep.

He had the most extraordinary dream.

He was himself, and he was not. He was simultaneously a man and something small, with long legs and papery wings. He ran through the halls of Glen Fae, that were at once normal-sized and gargantuan. Patches of moonlight were like vast silver fields in the infinite blackness. He dashed through the moonlight, wings fluttering.

There was someone running ahead. They kept disappearing around corners just as he was catching up, giving him only the barest glimpses: a swath of pale hair, the metallic flutter of wings. This only excited him further, and he went faster, lungs laboring, wings propelling him forward.

Stars glowed through the windows, close enough to pick like fruit, and dust motes the size of planets drifted by. The scent of the woman filled his senses, and he plunged forward, lunging around the corner onto the landing.

Glen Fae's great staircase opened before him, a space so vast it stretched beyond all senses. His quarry stood at the balcony railing, breasts rising and falling, wings snapping. She was paler than the moon, her skin absorbing light like a gemstone, and her hair was a fall of starlight. Her green eyes glowed. Her mandibles, so exquisitely sharp, twitching alluringly, filled him with desire.

The woman gazed at him with equal hunger. "Stephen," she sighed, her folded pincers reaching out.

He leaped for her, wings buzzing, forelegs lashing out.

Then he awoke.

He lay in the heart-pounding darkness, sweat cooling on his skin. The room spun around him. A dream. Just a dream. He was a human man, not some man-mantis thing, and he was in bed, not running around a gargantuan house in pursuit of a female of sharp-edged allurements…

He rolled over, pulling the blanket over his shoulder, while on his bedside table, the jade mantis gleamed.

***

"Well, good morning," said Mrs. Arden when Stephen stumbled into the kitchen. "Restless night?"

He braced himself against the counter. "You could say that." Through the kitchen window, the forest shifted, wavering like water. He closed his eyes against the daylight, filtering through muggy, humid clouds.

When it became obvious Mrs. Arden wasn't going to make him a cup of coffee—she was clearly still displeased with him—he groped for the percolator. Every movement felt unfamiliar, effortful. It was as if his body wasn't quite the right shape anymore—or as if he'd inhabited a different body last night and was no longer used to this one. The dream flashed through his head, and he had to shut his eyes again.

Corinne came tromping in. "Holy shit," she said when she saw him. "What happened to you?"

Stephen viewed his sister with even more disfavor than usual. After the pale woman last night, Corinne seemed frumpier and clumsier than ever. "Shouldn't you be going to work or something?"

"Summer break, bozo. One of the advantages of being a college professor." She put on the kettle for tea. "Seriously, though, Stephen, you look like shit. What'd you do, go on campus for a little weed?"

"No," he said, beginning ministrations with the coffee maker. "I just didn't sleep well."

There came a strange sound: a snickering laugh, mixed with an insectile buzz.

He jerked, the coffee maker lurching in his hands. His gaze was yanked up, and so he saw the praying mantis on the windowsill.

It stood just outside the window screen, antennae waving. It was as white as the jade statuette, as the mantis-woman in his dream, and when it twitched its mandibles, desire stabbed through him—

Revulsion slammed into him. "Get off!" He slapped the window screen, making it shudder. The mantis flicked its wings and took off, a buzz like papery laughter trailing from it.

"Damn thing…" He turned, breathing hard, to find the women staring at him.

Corinne stood frozen with her teacup in her hand, eyes wide and horrified, but Mrs. Arden's glasses gleamed, a strange smile tugging her lips…

"It's just a mantis, Stephen," she said mildly.

Stephen stared at her, words caught in his throat,

before stamping out of the kitchen without breakfast.

***

Stephen went to Marcus's room—whether to check on him or confront him, he wasn't sure—but Marcus was sound asleep, feeble hands resting on the counterpane, face wan and exhausted even in slumber. Stephen stood at his doorway a long moment before turning away.

No doubt it was due to lack of sleep and food, but he kept thinking he saw things. Shadows that moved in the corners of his eyes, tiny long-legged forms that leaped away. The corridor seemed to shiver with unseen motion as he walked through it. He thought again of his dream, running on multiple gossamer legs through this same hallway, so small the house seemed larger than a cathedral…

He waited until Mrs. Arden was out of the kitchen before going in to grab some food. Then he returned to his bedroom and tried to get some work done. But it was no good. His eyes kept straying beyond his laptop screen, to the humid garden through the windows, the forest beyond. He kept thinking he saw the movement of graceful, threadlike legs. The flash of white.

There was white on his computer screen. A white mantis's hooked forelimb, reaching out grotesquely from the abstract design he was creating. The hairs stood up on his neck. Why had he drawn that in? It in no way fitted his vision for this project.

Mouth dry, he erased it and started over.

At the window, white wings buzzed. A tiny triangular head cocked to the side; unblinking green eyes watched.

***

Dinner that evening was a strained affair. Corinne and Mrs. Arden were both giving Stephen the silent treatment, glaring at him around forkfuls. He ate in stubborn silence.

After dinner, he was glad to return to his room. He wondered if he would have more weird dreams tonight but dismissed the idea. It was just the one night, and surely it was only the strangeness of the dream that had kept him unsettled all day. There was nothing to worry about.

He did put the jade mantis away, though, locking it in its velvet bed inside the box. Not for any reason, really. Just to keep it safe.

He read on his phone until his eyelids grew heavy before snapping off the lamp.

The dream began almost immediately.

He was leaning on the rail over the vast stairwell. A glowing, flickering cyclone whirled in the dark stairwell, an undulating column of sparks. No, not sparks. Insects that were also people. Men and women beautiful enough to make mortals weep, pincers clicking, wings whirring out the song of the dance.

A white spark detached itself from the column. White Mantis landed on the rail, folding her wings beneath their cases. She looked at him with lidless green eyes, and her mandibles clicked within her secret smile.

Her scent was overwhelming.

Aflame with desire, he flung himself at her, spiky hooks spread wide. She leaped away laughing, and he flew after her, wings a blur. He crossed the unthinkable abyss of the stairwell, pursuing White Mantis into the swarm, her irresistible scent clear to his senses even through the buzzing gathering of the Others. They swooped and soared, Stephen and White Mantis, and the laughter of the Others rattled loud in their carapaces.

At last, she landed, spiraling down to the vast plain of the carpet at the bottom of the stairwell. She groomed herself, legs rubbing against her face, and her white breasts flashed like stars. He landed before her, six legs trembling, breath coming ragged.

She looked at him at last, head cocked. "Come, love," she said, voice like rasping velvet. "You have flown with me. Now dance with me."

He launched himself at her, his forelegs at the ready, but she was ready for him too. Her hooked legs caught his, and they dueled back and forth on the carpet, slashing and stabbing one another, each blow a jolt of pain and desire.

At last, she wrestled him down, her hooks jabbing over his shoulders and deep into his back. He writhed at the fearful ecstasy of her embrace.

"Yes," she murmured, leaning close. "Yes, you are mine now."

And, mandibles sharp, she lunged for the final kiss.

He jerked awake, head spinning.

Outside, the summer dawn was breaking, flooding the world with light and the songs of birds. And buzzing, singing insects, so many of them. But not like the Others, oh, no, not like White Mantis—

Stumbling out of bed, he made his way to the locked box. His hands trembled when he unlocked it again. There White Mantis lay, agleam in the morning light.

Taking out the statuette, he rubbed it against his chest, his face. The jade was so cool, so smooth. He'd never felt anything more erotic. He ran his tongue over the stone, taking in the cold taste. Gently, he bit it.

On his back, the wounds left by White Mantis stung, and a wet warmth trickled down his back.

***

There was a new scent in the air.

Stephen, sitting beside his father's bed, found himself inhaling it slowly and deeply. What *was* it? Like spice, wood, leaves, and earth, something that just evaded recognition. It emanated from the walls, the polished wood floors. It was as though all of Glen Fae was breathing, a living thing.

"Something on your mind, son?" Marcus eyed him from the bed.

"What's that smell?" Stephen sniffed in illustration

"The forests." Marcus's voice came out weak, and he coughed. "The Scottish forests where Robert Cameron felled the timber for this house and brought it across the sea. The American forests that furnished the rest of the wood." He broke off in another cough. "The house remembers."

"Houses can't *remember* things," said Stephen, but his scorn came out vague and absent-minded. His eye had been caught by the pattern of light and shadow on the carpet, where the tree branches waved and shifted, breaking up the sunlight, making shapes…

White Mantis opened her arms to him, arms of shadow and light and daggered spikes. The sunlight gleamed on her white hair, her white carapace.

A snore rose from Dad's open mouth. Stephen ignored it. He'd forgotten all about his dying father. His mind wandered, thoughtless as an insect flying through the summer afternoon.

He got to his feet; desire a hard, eager thing. The wounds White Mantis had given him last night sent exquisite lashes of pain through him. He licked his lips, watching her every move.

White Mantis stole up to Marcus's bed. She cocked her head, looking down at the sleeping man. Then she bent over to nibble her mandibles against his thin, wasted flesh.

"Not good eating now," she said in her velvet rasp. "Your mother should have devoured him long ago."

Stephen laughed aloud at this, and so did she, buzzing, trilling laughter.

He launched himself at her, flying over the bed, and they tumbled to the floor, weightless and soundless. Limbs tangled together, wings buzzing, he rubbed his head against hers, inhaling her incomparable scent. Then he lashed out with his forelegs, half-serious, half-playful, and they danced across the carpet, through the shifting bars of darkness and light.

***

"Are you all right, Stephen?" Mrs. Arden peered at Stephen's full dinner plate, glasses flashing. "You haven't been eating much these last few days."

He blinked in confusion. Days? What were 'days'? There were only gradations of light and darkness now, times when White Mantis emerged from moonlight and times when she emerged from sunlight and shadow.

Then an echo of human thought returned, and he remembered how time was partitioned in the human world. "Haven't been hungry, I guess," he said at last. His face itched, and he rubbed an arm across it.

Corinne stared at him from across the table. "You haven't been blinking much either. Is this some weird new diet? Lose weight through evaporation of your eyeballs?"

He sneered and blinked, slow and deliberate. The unfamiliar motion felt strange against his eyeballs, like sand being rubbed across his lenses.

Mrs. Arden sat back and regarded him a long

moment. A shadow of sorrow crossed her face. "I'd ask if you still intended to sell Glen Fae," she said quietly, "but I think it's already too late."

At this another human shadow fell over him: fear. "What do you mean?"

"Yeah." Corinne frowned at the housekeeper. "What do you mean, Mrs. Arden?"

"You'll find out." Mrs. Arden avoided their gazes as she stood, scraping her chair back, and began to clean up. He jolted with surprise when she leaned over to kiss him, light and soft, on the forehead. "Good night, Stephen."

He cocked his head at her, uncomprehending. Already human emotions were falling away again, forgotten, replaced by inhuman joy and expectancy, the absoluteness of purpose that no mortal sentient could comprehend. For tonight he would see White Mantis again, and that was all that mattered.

He left the kitchen, columnlike human legs clumping over the floorboards. The forest-shadows of the house fell around him like gentle shawls of cobweb. A fly flew past, a tiny spark of life, and he lashed out, smiling as his fingers closed on the struggling body.

He popped it in his mouth. Delicious.

***

Night fell completely, and silence reigned in Glen Fae. The stars gazed down with pitiless eyes, and the forest stirred, restless and expectant.

Dad slept the thin, restless sleep of the dying, his spirit ebbing away with every shallow, gasping breath. Mrs. Amelia Arden slept in the room next door, ready to care for him as needed, her glasses gleaming on her bedside table in the light of her alarm clock. Corinne, more unnerved by Glen Fae's recent shadows than she'd let on, had driven her car away after dinner and was not present at all.

Stephen did not sleep.

He danced instead, exulting in the strength of his hard-shelled, wiry body. Through the darkness of Glen Fae he leapt, silent and unnoticed, and around him the Others chittered and whirled too, eyes glittering, as lovely as the stars outside, and as soulless.

Stephen scented White Mantis and hurried on. He half-ran, half-flew down the corridor, the scents of the ancient forests swirling around him, until the vast spaces of the stairwell opened before him again.

The Others danced in a wavering, glittering column in the stairwell, a galaxy of tiny stars. But none could outshine White Mantis, clinging to the rail with four silken legs, her forelimbs folded, spines interlocking.

She gazed at him and waved her forelegs in invitation. "My love," she sighed. "My Stephen."

"My love." He stepped forward, human heart pounding, insect legs barely touching the carpet. "My White Mantis."

He waved his forelegs at her, the sign of submission and entreaty. She opened her arms to him and presented him her body.

The Others—all the Others who'd lived in Glen Fae since its construction, who'd watched the Cameron family for four hundred years, who'd noted the faithlessness of this generation's heir—all of them swarmed close, beautiful men and women, exquisite insects, and they watched to see what he would do, to see what their spell would do to the oath breaker, the faithless one, the betrayer of bargains.

Stephen climbed onto her back, legs easily finding purchase. He put his abdomen to hers and began the consummation of their long, drawn-out ritual.

And she, turning her face back in a perfect circle, opened her mandibles and chomped directly into his head.

The Others all danced and laughed with triumph, whirling in a glittering cloud. White Mantis finished her meal, eating Stephen's head like an apple, while her dying mate finished his duty.

When all was at last done, White Mantis spread her wings and flew away, into the great swarm of the Others. She let her mate's lifeless body fall, unnoticed.

Far away, there came a large, meaty thump.

***

Corinne didn't return until late the next morning, parking her car and stumbling up the drive, exhausted and still half-drunk from her wild night on the town. She struggled with the keys to the front door, cursing, the shadows of the summer forest casting wavering spots of light over the door and obscuring her vision.

She thought she smelled something funny as she finally swung the door open, and a rush of air came out. But she didn't realize what it was until she stepped inside and saw the headless, naked corpse of her brother lying on the carpet of the entryway.

Her scream woke Mrs. Arden upstairs, but not Marcus. He lay with a still, unbreathing chest and glassy, unseeing eyes, rigor mortis already setting in and a smile still on his lips.

***

Within the walls of Glen Fae, in their secret nests and hives, the Others buzzed and crooned, joy and contentment running through the swarm. They had dealt with the oath breaker and were safe once more. They ran adoring legs and antennae over White Mantis, who preened herself with great satisfaction. Her abdomen was already heavy with developing eggs.

Soon there would be more.

The Green Rail
Jenna Layton

"There. Nobody saw it," says Clark, using his paddle to drape a clump of frogbit over the partially-submerged sign that reads, 'private property–no trespassing.'

"Saw what?" asks Arjun with a grin.

Clark Thompson and Arjun Kumar, relatively young at forty-one and thirty-eight, have been treating this portion of the expedition as a one-sided race. They shot ahead of the gray-haired elders, Ross Grady and Sonny Watanabe, as soon as the tandem canoes entered the water, only occasionally slowing to scan the reed-lined edges of the marsh for signs of birds or other animals before taking off again.

Now, they turn to the older men while gesturing to their handiwork. Sonny gives them a thumbs-up; Ross, a wry salute.

As they wait for the two to catch up, Clark spots movement near shore. He raises his binoculars, while Arjun hefts his camera, which bears an intimidatingly large telephoto lens. Foraging in the water along the reeds is a small brown and gray bird with black and white markings and a bright yellow bill. It's a sora.

"Wouldn't it be funny if we saw it here and didn't have to trespass at all?" asks Clark.

"No kidding, we could just go back to the hotel and start celebrating," says Arjun, not taking his eyes off his camera's screen as he snaps photos of the sora.

It was a fine bird, but the men didn't journey out to a marsh in a Southern state for a sora. They didn't lie to their family members about where, exactly, they were going, for a sora. They didn't have strategy meetings where they scrutinized satellite images and talked EXIF data for a sora.

They're here for *Rallus smaragdus*: the green rail.

The small waterbird with striking chestnut and emerald feathers lived peacefully in the land that became America for countless years. Then the Swamp Land Act of 1850 struck, and its habitat was largely drained and developed. The scant remaining green rails were killed when late-Victorian fashion called for feathered hats.

Eventually, the green rail was considered extinct, written off like the ivory-billed woodpecker, Carolina parakeet. However, in the past few decades, sporadic sightings have been reported. Besides a few grainy photos and sound recordings, they are largely hard to verify. The birds are known to be solitary and infamously reclusive. They live deep in wetlands, only tentatively stepping out beyond the reeds. Like many other rails, chicks are born black and turn dark brown before reaching adulthood, leading to many hopeful observations that are later determined to be juveniles of another species.

Then came The Photo that led Clark, Arjun, Ross, and Sonny here. It was seemingly taken in the evening, showing water and reeds. There's a gap in the foliage like a doorway, and there stands an unmistakable green rail.

Even slightly out of focus, the photo would be a lifetime achievement for any birder. Strangely, it was posted under an alias, under an account with no history. To some birders' chagrin, it was posted on iNaturalist instead of eBird. Only a general location was given. The sighting blew up in the birding world, with desperate birdwatchers begging the faceless account for the coordinates.

Just three hours after the photo was posted, it disappeared, and the account was deleted.

Clark was one of those who thought to save the photo before it disappeared. His local birding group was excited by the story, but for most, it was a passing curiosity. Few in the group wanted to travel so far for a rarity sighting that might have been a hoax.

Of course, that didn't stop others. Masses of birders descended on wetlands in the wide area given. Enticingly, the photo contained one small clue: along the right edge, a few inches of a wooden structure poked into the frame. Was it a dock, a viewing platform, a houseboat? Birders scoured parks, open spaces, and private properties alike for the spot, angering rangers, conservationists, and the managers of various marinas. One pair of birders went missing. No one saw the bird, which many surmised had been frightened away by all the hubbub.

That was when Clark and Arjun started studying satellite photos. They mapped out where people had already searched, and at what else was in the area. At that point, the younger men broached the subject of an expedition with some of the most experienced birders in their group. Harriet, Ike, and Liz all demurred, citing their age and the likelihood of the supposed sighting being a hoax. Ross and Sonny, however, were all in, which seemed to bode well for the trip. After all, those two had lists most birders could only dream of. Ross photographed a thick-billed parrot in Mexico. Sonny once saw the critically endangered ʻākohekohe of Hawaii.

As the older men studied the satellite images, one location stood out to them. It was a remote, secluded habitat that some parts of the South would call a bayou, and its most striking feature in aerial photographs was a lake surrounded by dense vegetation. The lake was shaped like an egg, and at its narrower end, there was an island. On this island was a wooden structure, directly at the waterline.

Arjun found a years-old video of a vlogger visiting the island by kayak. He and Clark rewound the video several times to pause on the exact frame where the exterior of the building at the water's edge was shown. Although it had since further degraded from the elements, when they compared it to the wooden structure seen in the green rail photograph, it seemed to be an exact match. They had their location.

Then, they planned. The official story was that they were making a birding trip to one of the wetland nature preserves nearby. Ross and Sonny mapped out how they could reach the egg-shaped lake from a nearby open space. There would be some narrow passages through swampland, but they were sure they could do it with the right prep. They procured canoes, machetes, compasses, radios, water, provisions, first-aid kits, waders, and bird blinds. They were as ready as they could be.

While Arjun snaps photos of the sora, Clark notes a tricolored heron, which swoops down like a graceful blur of white, slate-blue, and burgundy to land on the purposefully obstructed sign.

He nudges Arjun.

Arjun starts to turn his camera toward this larger bird but stops. "Tris are my favorite heron, but we probably shouldn't have evidence that we saw the sign."

The thing about the place they're going is that they're not supposed to be there. No one is. It's private, corporate land, and it was the location of a busy salt mine until a sinkhole disaster destroyed the salt deposits, killed a dozen workers, and created the lake and island they mean to reach today. A smattering of adventurers have sought it out since then.

Old news articles reveal tragedies. There was a drowning fifteen years ago, and another three years ago. In both instances, groups ventured to the forbidden lake to party and swim. In the earlier instance, friends reported that the victim saw an alligator gar, tried to swim closer, and they lost sight of him. The more recent story is similar. A girl drinking with her friends on shore cried out that she saw a manatee, dove into the water for a better look, and was never seen again. It's thought the bodies disappeared into the caverns connected to the sinkhole. The articles warned of patrols guarding the area in the immediate aftermath.

For a green rail, though, trespassing is worth the risk. In the unlikely scenario that they are stopped by canoeing security guards or kayaking law enforcement, they feel secure knowing their group has two white guys. Besides, they're birders. What's less threatening than a small group of dorky birders, laden with binoculars and field guides? "Whoops, sorry, about that," they can have Ross or Clark say. "We didn't notice any signs. We thought we heard an American bittern and got excited."

And if they do see the rail, they have a plan. They'll strip their photos of all location data. They'll make sure to closely crop shots so as little of the surrounding area is shown as possible. They'll generalize the location they post on eBird and iNaturalist, and when pressed by other birders, they'll name the adjacent open space. If the

Department of Fish and Wildlife gets involved, which they probably would…well, they'll reveal the true location to the authorities, but they'll play dumb about how they ended up where they did. After all, people miss signs all the time. And they'd likely be forgiven. What's a small bit of trespassing in an abandoned marsh compared to finding solid evidence of a critically endangered bird? DFW would probably laud them as heroes while working to add the land to protected areas.

Truly, any amount of hounding would be a fair trade for observing the elusive green rail. For all of them, it would be a 'lifer,' which in birder parlance means a bird species they would be witnessing for the first time in their lives. Unless the ivory-billed woodpecker still exists, hidden in some deep forest, this might be the last chance for Ross and Sonny to get a lifer in the contiguous United States.

The four continue onwards. Soon, they get into the narrower channels of the swamp. Laden with Spanish moss, the towering trees filter the winter light. The water is thick with invasive water hyacinth.

"Did you know that at one point, the American government was thinking of using hippos to control this stuff?" Clark asks, poking at the floating plants.

"I've heard that," says Sonny. "They were hoping hippo burgers would catch on, too. Can't say it sounds appetizing, but I'd give it a try."

They then talk about the rumored hippos of Colombia, descendants of those brought to that country by drug lord Pablo Escobar.

"Imagine if we saw a hippo here," said Arjun.

It isn't that hard to believe. There's a sense that almost anything could feasibly emerge from the plant-covered water, and indeed they do spot several alligators. The giant reptiles glide through the water, only eyes and snouts visible, or else lie on hummocks like black logs.

"We probably won't see any hippos, but a manatee would be cool," says Clark.

"Just don't end up like that girl," Arjun says.

"There are plenty of reasons to not go in the water here, and one of them is at two o' clock," says Sonny, pointing with his paddle.

A long, dark shape undulates effortlessly along the surface, heading toward the first canoe.

"Shit," yells Clark.

Arjun seconds the comment, even as he whips out his camera.

The older men laugh. They've both been in this sort of environment before, seeking out birds like the white-crowned pigeon and purple gallinule, and they know what to watch out for.

"It's a cottonmouth," Ross says but doesn't bother to take out his camera. He's a bird man, through and through.

Clark waits for Arjun to get the perfect shot then gingerly nudges the venomous snake away with his paddle.

Farther up the river, however, they come across something that gives all of them pause.

At first, all they see is the limpkin up ahead. The heron-like, white-speckled brown bird is perched on something that elevates it above the vegetation. While Arjun and Ross take photos, Clark and Sonny glide the canoes in closer.

When they get to a bend in the channel, the limpkin is in a small cove off to the side, perched on a wooden rowboat.

They're all silent. The limpkin flutters away.

Finally, Clark states the obvious question. "Someone else is here?"

As they paddle closer, Arjun hums the banjo tune from *Deliverance* to break the tension. It doesn't work.

"It's been here for a while," Ross says when they get a better view. "Look at all the leaves and Spanish moss on it."

At least there's no evidence of competitors at this location today. But why has a boat been abandoned here, in the middle of nowhere? Ross speculates that maybe it drifted here in a storm, but Sonny points out that it is tied to the branches of a bush on shore.

Then they see the name of the boat in peeling paint: *The Albatross.*

"Isn't that the boat the two guys who went missing were in?" Clark asks.

Arjun nods, but adds, "but they were out at the state park."

"Unless they lied about where they were going. Just like us," says Sonny.

The words lie heavy in the air. If anything happens to them today, no one will know where to search for them.

The men paddle closer. In the abandoned boat, the oars are still present, as are a black jacket, an empty camera case, and a blue water bottle with bird poop on it.

"Do we report this to the Coast Guard?" Arjun asks.

Ross shakes his head. "We don't need to do that."

Clark speaks up. "But if it is the missing men's boat—"

"We don't know that this is the right boat. Any number of boats could be called '*The Albatross*.' Maybe there are some hillbillies living out here, and it's their boat," suggests Ross.

"Or poachers," says Sonny, his brow furrowed. "Could be there are saw palmettos nearby. Companies buy up the berries for bunk cures. Still…"

The men stare at the boat and at the swamp beyond.

From somewhere in the greenery is the haunting call of the limpkin, nicknamed the 'crying bird.'

"I bet you're right, Sonny," says Ross. "It's probably a poacher's boat, waiting for berry season."

The younger two men look less certain, but the truth is that neither wants to end their quest early.

"We can look up the articles about the missing men when we get back to civilization," says Sonny. "Those will surely have pictures or a description of the boat. If this is the same boat, we can call it in as an anonymous tip."

This sounds wise and sensible, and the others nod, relieved that they can go forward with their consciences clear.

The journey continues in silence—from the men, if not the surrounding animals. Bugs and frogs chirp. There are the shrill whines of common gallinules, the trills of palm warblers, and the shriek of a green heron. The environment feels wilder, more dangerous. The older two men think about their lists of birds—both handwritten and on eBird—and about how long it's been since they could add a new species. Finding the green rail would be their legacy.

The younger men think about hillbillies hiding in the swamp, and about whether there might be bodies out there, rotting. Clark's wife told him before he left not to do anything stupid. It's only now that he thinks that maybe, this might qualify.

But gradually, Clark and Arjun's minds, too, turn back to the green rail. Getting solid evidence of this bird would make them important. Clark imagines speaking gigs with conservation groups. Arjun pictures his photograph of the bird being named one of the most notable photographs of the year.

That's not to say that the men think only of glory for

themselves. No one goes into birding for glory. People go into birding for the need to witness, to know. The men want to observe this bird, this reportedly beautiful green-and-brown bird, thought to have been made extinct due to human greed and foolishness. They want to know that it survives, that out there in the wildernesses across the world, birds still survive.

When they reach the egg-shaped lake, they find it barred off with barbed wire. It's strung up along the trees bordering the lake that was formed by disaster. Despite their extensive preparations, none of them brought wire-cutters. Fortunately, someone else did. They don't have to circle far until they find a place where the wires have been snipped through. The cuts are rusty though—they've been there awhile.

Once past the wire, they're paddling into the lake proper. They've entered at the widest part of it.

"We're going over the sinkhole now," says Clark. "It's over a hundred feet deep. Somewhere down there in the caverns are likely the bodies of the people who drowned."

They glance down as if skeletons might be visible, but all they can see is the murky water.

"Those mine workers, too," adds Sonny.

"What a way to go," says Ross. "I wonder if they even knew what hit them."

Across the lake, in the narrow and shallower end, is the island with the dilapidated building. It was one of the mine's administration buildings, and it's the only structure in the immediate area that didn't disappear into the sinkhole.

"Look," says Clark as they get closer. He holds up his phone, which doesn't have service, but does have the saved photo from iNaturalist. "It's a perfect match."

They sit in the boats for a few minutes, discussing

strategy. They've brought camouflaged tarps to form bird blinds. Perhaps one or two of the canoes can be set up as floating blinds. The ruined building also has windows—depending on the condition inside, it might be a good plan for one or two of them to set up scopes from there.

Sonny and Ross are hashing out the pros and cons of each spot and who should be where when Arjun lets out a gasp.

"Guys," he hisses.

The other three follow his gaze.

There, swimming placidly not too far away, is a green rail. Even though none of them have ever seen one before, it's immediately recognizable. This specimen looks straight out of a *Sibley Guide*, but even better. Its face, neck, wingtips, and breast are a bright, lush green. Its back is deep chestnut, much like the plumage of a cinnamon teal, but flecked with black like other rails. The bill and eyes are a matching orange.

Arjun and Ross have their cameras up in an instant. Sonny has his binoculars, and Clark, even though he told himself earlier he'd leave the photography to the pros, starts snapping photos on his phone.

The rail is unbothered by their presence. It dallies through the water unhurriedly, its upright, triangular tail sticking up like a comically small shark fin.

It's an even better view than John Salva had. John was the person who posted the blurry photo on iNaturalist. He had gone out alone to try to find the green rail, and when he saw it standing in the reeds, his hands shook with excitement as he took the photo. He didn't post it until several days later, though. The shock had lessened by then, the adrenaline spike from his frantic race from the lake subsiding, but his mind was still a haze of confusion over what he had seen. He eventually decided to post the photo anonymously, then, overwhelmed by the attention and plagued by paranoia, deleted it.

But sitting in their canoes, Clark, Arjun, Ross, and Sonny don't know any of that. They can't believe their luck. All this way they traveled, unknowing if this gamble would pay off, and this moment is more than worth it. They've seen the bird. They've seen its breathing, moving form, its beautiful feathers. Seeing it like this is so much different than a faded, stuffed specimen in a museum. Now they know that the green rail still exists.

And they will be birding legends. They can write that name, *Rallus smaragdus*, in their lists. They can report the sighting online and brace for the rush of disbelief, excitement, and jealousy. They can tell other birdwatchers this story for years to come.

The bird raises its head. The birders think it might be about to let out a call, but something else happens instead. The bill thickens. The head and neck thicken. The brown and green start intermingling and growing duller as the surface of the bird almost seems to liquify, taking on the texture of octopus skin.

The men can't move. The older two think that perhaps they are having a stroke.

The bird, or what was in the shape of the bird, stretches, expands. More and more of it rises from the water. It looks like a rotting log at one moment, then like a column of water, then like an anaconda, or a fuzzy photo of the Loch Ness Monster. There is no recognizable head, however, just a strange shape, undulating and massive. As it rushes toward the two canoes in a silent strike, along with the usual thoughts of terror, disbelief, and flashes of their lives and loved ones, every single one of the men also feels a bit of disappointment.

They have not seen the green rail, after all.

What Aria Found in the Swamp
J. Neira

It was the third morning in a row she'd woken from a nightmare, her skin slick with sweat and her mind scrambling to distinguish between dream and reality.

She sat up, still trying to grasp at the dream that was slipping through her fingers like grains of sand and pushed away the cotton sheets that had turned damp from the draught creeping into the room. Rain continued to patter against the windows, but it was a light drizzle compared to last night's ferocious downpour and howling wind.

Taking a moment to catch her breath, she slipped out of bed, her bare feet curling against the cold wooden floor, and padded to the window to pull aside the curtains. Hazy sunlight seeped into the room, illuminating the dust mites that stirred through the air.

She looked at the land behind the house. The grass was matted down and waterlogged from the rain, and the trees were windswept, their branches tangled together and trailing limply against the stone wall that circled the property. Just beyond the tree line was the swamp, hidden from sight, and she could only imagine what kind of foul-smelling sludge the storm had dredged up.

Leaving the curtains billowing behind her, she crossed the room, catching a glimpse of herself in the worn wooden mirror. There was an ashen hue about her, and heavy shadows clinging to the skin beneath her eyes, but what caught her attention the most was the strands of grey amongst her thick brown hair.

She stepped closer to the mirror, tugging absently at the discoloured hair, as though expecting it to fall out at her touch.

Grey hair wasn't exactly common at her age of twenty-three, and she wondered if it had something to do with the nightmares, and the stress she'd been under recently. It had to have been. Hair turned grey from stress, and she'd been more stressed than usual for the past several months. She hoped she'd be able to save at least some of her natural brown hair.

Trying not to dwell on it, she slipped into the adjoining washroom and cleaned off the sweat she'd accumulated in the night, pulling her hair back into a long braid that trailed over her shoulder.

Once she was dressed—in her familiar soft cotton pants and blue tank top—she grabbed a piece of fruit from the bowl downstairs and headed into the morning.

The rain had finally dispersed. Plink, plink came the steady dripping of water from the gutters outside the house.

Sinking her teeth into the soft flesh of the fruit, she lifted her face and let herself enjoy the dewy scent of the morning. The grass was soft and squelchy as she headed behind the back of the house, her shoes sodden with murky water by the time she reached the rear of the property. The wooden overhang at the back of the house had at least kept her logs dry, but it was starting to rot in several places, the roof becoming soft and brittle, ready to cave-in with one last battering.

Hauling a dozen thick logs onto the raised porch, she grabbed the woodcutting axe and began to split them with swift, practiced movements. The rhythmic thunk, thunk of the axe hitting wood soothed her, and she worked until her forehead glistened with sweat, and there was a pleasant ache in her muscles.

Straightening her back, she wiped the perspiration from her brow and began to stack the chopped logs beneath the overhang, ready to use as fuel for tonight's fire.

Thick tangles of vines had started to creep along the brickwork of the house, and a cluster of weeds and nettles had forced their way through the cracks in the concrete, their tall, wiry stems almost snagging at her ankles as she trod past them.

She tried to use her axe to sever them at the roots, but the blade was too thick to reach, so she gave up. If she recalled correctly, she had some other tools stored in the shed behind the house which might work more effectively.

After a moment's hesitation, she took her axe with her. From the rumours in town, there'd been a lot of people going missing recently, disappearing without a trace. It was enough to make anyone wary.

The storm had brought out the worms, and as she headed further away from her house, the more there seemed to be, their small pink bodies writhing amid the mud and wriggling along the path. She tried to step over as many as she could.

Following the stone wall that bordered her property, something snagged her attention: a lamppost on the other side of the wall, where several sheets of paper were fluttering in the breeze. There were more than she remembered.

Leaning against the wall, she studied the posters stapled to the post. The ink had started to run from the rain, but she could discern enough to know that someone else had gone missing. A hunter in his mid-thirties never came home to his family. His poster sat among many of a similar nature. Hunters, fishermen, woodcutters, foragers… All had vanished without a trace, leaving behind families who were worried about them. It wasn't natural. Something was going on, but nobody knew what. The village was already small in number, and with all these disappearances, it was starting to feel more and more empty. Abandoned.

She raised her glance to the top of the new MISSING poster, where someone had scrawled in bright red ink: YOU DESERVE IT!

A frown formed between her brows. There was no need for slander, not when people were in mourning. Some local kids were probably responsible, uncaring of the consequences.

Leaving the posters fluttering somberly behind her, she hefted her axe and headed towards her shed, half-hidden amongst the copses of trees. Several branches had broken off during the storm, and the roof of the outbuilding was littered with wet, soggy leaves. It would take a few days for the mess to clear up, but it could've been worse. At least, there'd been no structural damage to repair. She was handy with garden tools, but that was the extent of her skills when it came to being self-reliable.

The door to the shed was locked with a heavy padlock, the metal stained red with rust. She kept the key hidden beneath a rock nearby, since she was often forgetful about bringing the key with her whenever she left the house.

The storm had turned the soil into a thick sludge, and she grimaced as she kicked over a rock to find a clump of worms wriggling and squirming underneath, their slimy bodies slithering over each other. She quickly replaced the stone and tried another, until she caught a glint of silver among the dirt. When she crouched to retrieve the key, something else stole her attention.

A thick cluster of long, rubbery green strands threaded through the undergrowth. They didn't look like weeds or vines, and she didn't remember seeing them before, either. There was something almost grotesque about the way they trailed limply along the ground, matted with soil and dirt. Curious, she touched one of them, curling her fingers around the strange, almost elastic texture. When she tugged on it, it resisted but from far away, and when she followed the threads with her eyes, they disappeared deeper into the trees. What were they, and where were they coming from? They were unlike anything she'd seen before.

Pocketing the key to the shed, she stood and stared into the forest. Beneath the thick canopy of leaves, it was dark among the trees. The rain had soaked into the ground and made the soil claggy, and there was a smell of damp undergrowth and moss that wasn't entirely unpleasant. Shadows swelled between the boughs, and for a moment, she thought of all those missing people posters. She clenched the axe tighter in her hand, her palms growing sweaty. She could return to the house, or she could follow those mysterious green fibers into the unknown.

Despite the prickle of warning at the back of her neck, she took a step forward, her shoes sinking into the ground.

An image flashed across her mind, unbidden. It was from a dream, buried somewhere in the dark recesses of her memory, showing a waterlogged forest, silent and unmoving. Was this the same forest from her dreams—the one that had haunted her nightmares?

She shook her head, loose strands of hair tickling her cheek from where they'd escaped her braid. Surely, she was overthinking things. All forests appeared the same. She saw this one every time she peered out of her window, so it wasn't unusual for it to crop up in her dreams sometimes too.

The moment she stepped fully beneath the canopy, it was like the world went quiet. Everything had a hushed, muted quality to it in the forest. There was no bird call, no bugs chittering, nothing but the faint rustle of leaves, and the sodden squelch of her feet.

She scanned the shadows fervently, every glimpse of movement sending her heart spiking, but it was just the trees, their branches scraping together in the wind.

The filament trailed along beside her feet, barely visible in the gloom. She wondered briefly where they would lead her as she took hold of one, the texture slimy against her skin. She used it like a rope, following it through the densely packed trees.

The deeper she went into the forest, the stronger the smells grew. The musky scent of decaying leaves and rotten wood, and something else, bitter and putrid that almost made her eyes water. Was it the swamp? Was that where these strange green vines were leading her to?

Still holding onto the fibrous strands, something tugged it forward, raking it across her palm.

What the hell?!

With a start, she dropped it in disgust and peered at the clump of them. They crawled a few inches along the ground, then fell still again.

Were they…alive? Or was someone else causing them to move?

She swallowed back the lump in her throat, casting a

glance over her shoulder. The trees almost seemed to have closed in on her, and she'd lost sight of her house. There was nothing but darkness all around, interspersed with rot and decay.

She had to keep going.

Swapping the axe to the other hand, she wiped her sweaty palm down the front of her pants and steadied her breathing before treading onward.

The familiar sound of gushing water was somewhere ahead. Finally, she reached a brook. It was nothing but a small stream of clear water running through the trees ahead of her, but it meant she was getting closer to the swamp.

She paused by the water and dipped her hands into the cold current, splashing her face. Water dripping from her lashes, refreshed and more confident to keep going, she hopped over the brook to continue deeper into the trees.

She smelled the swamp before she saw it. The pungent, sulfuric gases emitted from the marshland surged through the trees like a tidal wave, making her stomach clench with nausea. The canopy above her had begun to thin out, allowing small pockets of grey light to dapple the ground below. Relieved to be out of the gloom, she searched the ground for the strands and traced them with her eyes to the very edge of the forest.

She'd been right from the start; they did lead to the swamp.

When she finally broke the tree line, she threw up a hand to shield her eyes from the hazy light, a sharp contrast to the forest. The air was heavy with the stench of the swamp, and flies buzzed and swarmed around her, their wings brushing past her skin and making her itch.

The bog lay in front of her, waterlogged and choked with weeds. The storm had dredged up all the silt and vegetation lying dormant at the bottom of the swamp, and it now lay in murky clumps on top of the water. Algae formed a thick layer across most of the surface, old tree roots and stumps rising from the water like corpses.

The deep, guttural croak of a toad was somewhere among the undergrowth, and the chirp of bugs and insects scuttled through the scrub.

The smell was eye-wateringly pungent, and she had to fight back the bile that burned up her throat, her stomach roiling.

As she turned her gaze away from the swamp, that's when she saw it.

It was hard to tell exactly what she was beholding. Some kind of hulking mass at the very edge of the swamp, covered in the same rubbery green strands that she'd followed here.

It was moving; shuddering and heaving, like something alive. It was making noises, too; gurgling and popping, belonging to something wet and slimy.

She raised her axe, gripping it with both hands as she took a step closer to the mass, her mind scrambling to understand what it was.

Barely visible beneath the green strands, she traced the curve of a head, the slope of shoulders, the bulge of a stomach... It was a person. No, not a person, but something with the shape of a human—the body of some kind of large, deformed creature. Behind it was what remained of a small stone house, nothing but half a structure and mounds of dust and debris. Pieces of old, rotten wood and fabric jutted from the ruins.

Every part of her body was screaming for her to get out of there. Whatever this thing was, it wasn't natural. But she continued drawing closer, raking her gaze over the hulking body as she tried to make sense of it all.

Those twisting green fibers were its hair. It was

draped over most of the creature's body, but between them, she caught the glimpse of a face. Something about it vaguely resembled a female, if such a thing could have a gender.

All that was visible was wrinkled grey skin that looked more akin to a prune, and large black lips that were puckered into a kiss. Farther up were the eyes, hollow and deep-set, closed against the light. Even though its eyes were shut, she had the sense that the creature was aware of her standing there.

With another full-bodied shudder, the creature started to move, its limp green hair falling away to reveal more of its wrinkled grey face. It was making those strange sucking noises again. It was eating something, its mouth puckering and clenching like it was tasting something delicious.

Repulsion and disgust battled her desire to flee. She paused at the edge of the swamp, her shoes sinking into the waterlogged ground, pulling her deeper into the earth. How long had this thing been here, so close to her house? Had the storm brought it out of the swamp, dragged it from the depths like some forbidden, arcane horror, or had it always been here, creeping in the shadows?

The creature gurgled again, and she watched with mounting dread as something red began to spill from its open mouth. Blood. The smell that followed was like nothing she'd experienced before, something sickly sweet yet sour at the same time, like a corpse that had been rotting for too long in the ground.

Something else began to emerge from the creature's mouth then; long and pale, covered in blood and saliva.

A human leg. It had been chewed on, the skin and muscles torn to shreds, exposing the white glint of bone beneath.

It fell out of the creature's mouth, landing amongst

the undergrowth, and she couldn't hold back her nausea anymore. She vomited onto the ground beside her, bile burning the inside of her cheeks. When she was finished, she wiped her mouth with the back of her wrist.

She froze. The creature's eyes were open, staring at her with two gleaming black shards of obsidian.

All those missing people… Is this where they'd ended up? In the stomach of this grotesque creature? Would she be next?

She gritted her teeth, gripping her axe tightly between her hands.

The creature let out a low, guttural groan that seemed to come from the back of its throat, its lips opening and closing, revealing a mouth full of wickedly sharp teeth, pieces of skin and blood trapped between the gums.

As it started writhing and moving towards her, she raised the axe over her head and brought it down with a heavy thunk, cutting through the strands of hair that were draped along the ground at her feet.

The creature let out another guttural moan, recoiling in pain when she sliced off another chunk of hair, the green strands withering up as soon as they were severed from its head.

With the creature distracted, she pulled free of the mud that was bogging her down, and rushed towards it, swinging her axe.

The sharp blade connected with something soft and slimy, and dark red blood spurted out in an arc, splashing across her cheek.

With a throaty cry, the creature tried to scramble away, but she brought the heel of her foot down, stomping hard on its stomach. Its soft flesh gave way beneath her shoe, and something warm and wet splattered up her leg, momentarily throwing her off balance.

She staggered back, panting heavily as she wiped the

blood from her cheek, trying not to retch from the smell.

Its body was starting to disintegrate into foul-smelling fluids, dark blood and stomach acid seeping into the surrounding marsh, pieces of regurgitated, half-dissolved body parts flooding out after it.

With clumps of its hair destroyed, she glimpsed more of the creature's face. Its skin sagged like melting candle wax, and small slits around its throat reminded her of the gills on a fish, making her wonder if it had emerged from the swamp, after all. Its black eyes, glistening like wet rocks, were half-closed in pain, and it had black lashes that looked like spider's legs, long and spindly.

Without a single ounce of remorse for the pitiful creature, she hefted her axe and tore into its face with a flurry of desperate slashes, tearing through skin and muscle, until there was nothing but a bloodied, mangled mess remaining.

It collapsed at the edge of the swamp, carrion flies already swarming around the corpse and feasting on its decaying flesh.

She staggered backwards, overcome with a crushing wave of fatigue. Now that the creature was dead, would that stop the disappearances? Had all those people really been eaten by this swamp monster? She wouldn't be able to say for sure, not until someone else went missing.

The foul smells and thick, muggy atmosphere of the swamp were starting to make her light-headed, and she fumbled away from the water, her ankles twisting over the tangled undergrowth.

The dizziness grew stronger, and she'd barely reached the tree line when her knees buckled, the ground giving way beneath her. Her vision began to swim, shadows encroaching along the edges, until everything went dark and quiet.

***

When she came to, Aria was lying on her back, staring up at the grey sky. Damp grass tickled her cheek, and something was crawling along her bare arm, leaving a wet, slimy trail along her skin.

With a soft groan, she sat up, the movement jolting her head and making it spin.

Clutching her head between her hands, she looked at herself. The front of her tank top was covered in dark blood, and the hem of her trousers were soaked with foul-smelling sludge. A small, grey-coloured worm was crawling along her arm, until she flicked it off with a shudder.

The swamp… And the creature… It had all been real. Not just another nightmare.

With a start, she glanced up, her vision swimming into focus. She half-expected to find herself still at the swamp, the creature's rotten remains steaming behind her, but she wasn't. She was lying on the grass in her backyard, close to where she'd been chopping wood earlier that day.

How had she gotten back? Had she somehow walked, without any memory of it? Or had someone brought her? But that didn't seem likely, and as she glanced around, there was no sign that she wasn't alone.

Taking a moment to regain her breath, she gingerly climbed to her feet. She grimaced as soreness shot through her body. There were leaves and twigs sticking out of her braid, and a little black beetle was crawling along her chin.

She brushed it all away.

Somewhere on the other side of those trees was the corpse of a creature that didn't belong on this earth. Would anyone believe her if she told them? Did she even believe it herself? If it wasn't for the blood on her clothes, maybe she wouldn't. Maybe she would rationalise it as some kind of absurdly vivid dream.

Before she headed inside, she searched for her axe, but it was nowhere to be seen.

Maybe she'd left it by the swamp or somewhere in the forest. It didn't matter now. It was over. At least, it should have been. But for her, her mind never moved on from that day.

For the next several weeks, her dreams were haunted by the creature. Memories of blood and darkness, of secrets hidden in the very depths of the swamp, plagued her. She began to dread the night, for it was in the shadows, with only the sickle moon for company, that the events of that day resurfaced.

In the clutches of midnight came the drip of stagnant water and the gurgling moan of something inhuman. She would smell the swamp as though it was right outside her window, the carrion flies buzzing around the rotten flesh of the creature she slayed.

She never went back to the swamp, to check if the creature had been real, or if it was really dead. Nobody else from the town went missing, but the mystery behind those disappearances was never truly solved; the families never found their solace. Only she knew the truth, but it was a truth that nobody else would believe.

It was a truth that haunted her to the very depth of her soul.

The Magnolia Tree
Cliff McNish

Around my fortieth birthday I got a promotion and ended up in a different branch of my insurance office. The morning walk to the train station took me down Inkerman Street and passed a tree.

It was a small tree, waist height, more of a bush, really. A magnolia.

I doubt I'd have even noticed it except for the poem. A verse stuck with a pin to the magnolia's slim dark trunk:

Yesterday was the best day of my life.
Thanks for sharing it with me.
Thank you for being so amazing and free.
Thank you for being my wife.
(There, I've written a poem, and you said I never
would! Simon. x)

The simple, heartfelt words made me smile. But they were intended for someone else, so I strolled on to the station.

That evening, however, I couldn't resist checking to see if the note was gone.

It was, and in the brimming, evening shadows, the Magnolia Tree's leaves stood proudly erect. I imagined a newlywed couple fondly passing love notes to each other, designating the tree their special location. Very romantic.

Two days later, I discovered another piece of paper attached to the trunk. Sticky tape had been used this time, and I'll admit I was a little voyeuristic when I peeked.

Handwritten in blue biro, the note *said:*
"Hi, Henny, hope you got the flowers. I didn't mean it. XXXX" Followed by a sorry smiley face.

So not a love poem this time. More a lover's regret after an argument. But it *was* an apology, and the kisses were a nice touch. The same couple? Possibly. But I doubt it because over the new few weeks I made a bizarre discovery: that people from all walks of life were unburdening their deepest feelings on the Magnolia. Fascinatingly, too, the notes were always attached to that single tree. No other trees in the area were being used–I checked.

Many sentences left on the Magnolia made me blush. Young lovers leaving nothing to the imagination. Old lovers equally passionate. People sincerely, often feverishly, in love. The tone was sometimes that of longing or regret, but always the subtext was love. Love tender, love fierce, love adamant.

I shouldn't have been reading any of these intensely personal reflections. I didn't over-censure myself for it, however. It's not as if I tampered with the notes or hung around to see who was leaving them. I allowed people their privacy. Sometimes, I'll admit, I'd fantasize that one of the poems was addressed to me. Or that *I* was the one who'd written the poem and had someone special in my life, desperately waiting for me to return home. It was nice to daydream. I'd never had much luck with relationships, and I was lonely. The notes helped to fill that gap. I'd take quick phone-pics of what was pinned to the bark, then hurry away before I was discovered.

The Magnolia flourished over time, and to check its contents more easily I sold my flat, buying a home on Inkerman Street. I also started transcribing the lovers' messages into a leather-bound Rowton's journal. Within only three months, I'd used every line up and had to buy another. By the start of my second year of recording entries, I'd filled three journals.

Was I jealous of all the heartfelt affection intended for others?

Yes. But what I experienced more strongly was a duty of care. People fall in and out of love. Without me to record them, most of these endearments would have been forgotten or lost over time, and it felt wrong to discard such precious feelings. Didn't the world need more love? Didn't we all deserve to be surrounded by such desires and hopes, even if we weren't the object of them? The *beautiful utterances*, I started calling them in my fourth year of collecting–a stuffy and formal name for notes typically written in white-hot passion, but so what? I was the scribe, the recorder; I could call them what I liked.

Two more years passed, and the passionate letters, jottings, and verses pinned or hung from the Magnolia Tree multiplied. I ended up clearing out my entire study to make room for extra journals, and meantime the Tree itself prospered. With each year, it grew taller and broader, until it was far bigger than any magnolia tree I'd seen, its trunk strident, the oversized tepals of its blossoms, the girth of engorged penises. Every April, the blossoms appeared with almost lurid haste, lasting only a few weeks before they faded.

More time passed, and somehow, I tipped over into my sixtieth birthday. Over a twenty-year period, I'd had opportunities to move from Inkerman Street, but never quite got round to it. It would have meant leaving the Magnolia Tree behind, or at least visiting it less often, and as the summers passed, I was less inclined to do so.

Other residents of Inkerman Street felt the same way. I couldn't recall any *For Sale* notices going up in recent years. Quite the opposite. Prices for even single basement rooms had skyrocketed.

It was with Maggy–a woman who knocked on my door like so many others, asking me if I'd let a room in my flat–that I might have had a chance of my portion of love at last. She was the same age as me, sixty-six, and seemed almost as shy. The trouble was that I didn't love her. Not enough, anyway, to leave a love couplet on the Magnolia Tree. I tried to conjure the urge, but the words fell dead under my fingers.

It meant I hit my seventies still alone, but I don't want that to conjure an image of sorrow in your mind. When I was lonely, I'd stare at the Magnolia Tree. Or I'd open one of my journals. I had hundreds, by now. Every room was stuffed with them.

Retirement suited me. I missed people at work, but not as much as I expected. The handful of friends I had were mostly casual acquaintances, and gradually I lost touch with them altogether. It was an austere life, I suppose, bound to the Tree, but I preferred things that way. My conversations had become desultory anyway, mostly restricted to *thank yous* at my local supermarket checkout counter. Glass-eyed assistants, their slack gazes lifted to the ever-growing shadow of the Magnolia, would offer me vague, monosyllabic responses.

Their lack of interest in an old man didn't bother me. They had better things to do, after all. There were such a lot of young people in our neighborhood these days. I saw them every day making love on the lawns, often hundreds at a time on warmer evenings. The men would be barely spent, still half-erect, as they lurched across to the Magnolia Tree to write their hasty, intense notes. I didn't know these young people, but I imagined them hurrying home from work, washing their grubby hands–even if they were clean, they'd fastidiously scrub them raw before holding their pens–and conjuring up something suitably sensitive. Flames of love most never guessed they had in them. Because, like me, their real life was now an inner life. An inner holiness.

I celebrated my eightieth birthday by gorging myself on journal entries. I had over two thousand journals now. My loft extension was packed to the rafters with the beautiful utterances. No one else celebrated my birthday with me. Even so, I closed the door to my study. I'd got into the habit of doing that in recent years. I'm not sure why. It was just me and the journals and, looming behind, in everlasting background, the vast healthy breathing trunk of the Tree.

The Magnolia was a wondrous sight to behold these days. All that ardently penned love, all that fervid passion pressed to its dry bark, had made the Tree so drunk with affection that its spreading roots could no longer be contained. They had long since ruptured the tarmac of Inkerman Street, making it impossible for traffic to navigate. Mothers trundling pushchairs could only bring their children up to the trunk, never beyond it. Sometimes, the toddlers inside those pushchairs clumsily held their first pens, writing on their wrists or scraps of leaf meaningless characters and letters that would later become so poignant.

The spread of the Magnolia had long ago destroyed most of the homes on the street. The destruction was welcomed. Those families lucky enough to live in homes whose walls, doors, and windows were breached rarely left their residences. They would merely lean against the swelling branches, occasionally leaving beautiful offerings.

A tradition began, enacted every April. It involved the men, straight or queer or whatever they chose to identify as, standing against the Tree while it was in blossom, seeding it with their arousals. Meantime the women would sew their pubic hair into patterns resembling the irregular spiraling tepals of the Magnolia Tree.

One time a stranger to the area fought past the gnarled root system blocking the entrance to Inkerman Street. I'm not sure how he managed it, but he came with a kid clinging to his shoulders. A boy was six, maybe seven, years old. The Magnolia Tree's lowest branches rested at a good height for a child that age to swing from, and when I saw him from my bedroom window, he looked like he was having a fun time.

I never saw him again. Nor his father. I didn't ask after them, either. It's not as if I was personally involved in the guarding of the Magnolia. That sort of activity was for the young lovers and poets of Inkerman Street.

Over the years, I suppose we residents all became, in our own fashion, ardent advocates for the Tree. We weren't entirely a community of gentleness and love, though. The street occupants argued continuously. Deaths became commonplace, and everyone aimed to be present to witness them. A great deal of fine poetry got written over those dramatic deaths. Other pacts were made, husbands cuckolded, daughters slain and written about, but mostly it was the lovers who prevailed. Paramours queued from dawn to dusk to leave their unique poems on the Magnolia Tree. The queues were orderly, dozens of lines often running right to the end of the street. But it was a silent street. Those waiting in line rarely spoke to one another. They were too intent on synthesizing their own private affections. Men with tactless, maladroit minds grew their locks like Keats and wept joyfully over dreary sunsets.

Sometimes joining the queues meant tough decisions–leaving elderly relatives or children they were responsible for at home. You'd hear the dependents crying in the night. Starved cries. Thirsty cries. It wasn't hard to hear their plaintive voices over the silence of the queues. Occasionally, inspired by the pathos, someone might add a line to their own verse-in-creation. But nobody ever broke rank to leave a queue once they joined. The slots were too precious. No-one ever kept your place or offered you theirs.

By the time I was nearing my ninetieth birthday, the Tree's roots were a tumescent hill-scape. They riddled not just Inkerman Street, but every street, road, and mews in the area. Colossal and regal, stuffed with our richest feelings, bloated with our magnanimity, the Tree was like a broad mushroom in its essential shape, and each spring it shed blossoms the weight of car doors. The fights to earn a spot to die under the great, off-white tepals started as early as mid-summer the previous year.

But all that heartfelt emotion came at a cost. Despite its prodigious size, the Magnolia Tree couldn't possibly handle all the notes clamorously attached to it. Over time, a precedence system arose whereby the conscientious early risers–those who stood in line longest, and were prepared to sacrifice more, sever a written-upon finger, thumb or toe–were prioritized. The people still using only paper for their poems ended up forlornly waiting years in line, without understanding why they never got any closer to the Magnolia.

It also became customary not just to inscribe the declarations and stanzas of the beautiful utterances on one's own skin, but to cut the patches off by knife or sharpened fingernail in clear public display. No adhesives were needed to pin those offerings to the Tree. Blood-wetted skin clung surprisingly well.

Scale mattered more and more. Charming little notelets and single-stanza exclamations of love were out. Epic orations were in. You knew the people who truly cared, because they were prepared to use their own internal organs to finish their poems. By cauterizing certain wounds, you could last a reasonable amount of time while inscribing a kidney, gall bladder, or stomach lining. The Magnolia Tree didn't seem to mind that the sentiments from such people were shorter or diluted in effective meaning toward their conclusions as their owners fell unconscious. It was purity of intention that counted. Only last month, dozens were crushed when the April blossoms fell. Right up to the last moment the lucky chosen citizens were darting glances at one another, the competition not to flinch fierce as the blossoms swayed above them like clangorous cathedral bells.

What does it mean to sacrifice for love? Somewhere around my ninety-third birthday, a middle-aged man used a hunting knife tore all the closely written skin off his legs. The miraculous part was not the act of sabotage itself, but that he achieved it in one continuous strip. I've no idea how he managed to carve around his groin without losing concentration. Sheer willpower, I suppose. Sheer love. Watched by everyone in queue '65,' he penned a few excruciatingly short couplets on his scrotum. Luckily, he'd written out the full poem (to his cat, I think, very touching) on his legs *before* he started cutting, because the fluid loss was so great he'd barely draped his glistening lower torso across the Magnolia's trunk before he bled out.

It was so impressive that the next person in the queue waited a full minute before trudging forward to make their offering.

But–can I say this, do I dare? –in the end, the Tree was just a tree. As vast as it was now and even making use of all available branch-space, there was no way to handle the sheer volume of daily offerings.

The first person to allow herself to be written upon by others–Sandy Cleavy, her name was–left her three kids in the house, walked to the Tree, and arranged her limbs wide apart against its trunk. She did it somewhat in the style of a snow angel. I'd moved into my flat overlooking the Magnolia Tree more than fifty years before, and it was weird, at first, seeing the beautiful utterances being pinned not to the Tree but Sandy's exposed flesh.

I think her steadfastness helped. Through rain or shine she just lay there, naked, her arms and legs spread wide. When room on those ran out, she offered her thighs, toenails and buttocks. When those areas were full, she gave permission for her genitalia to be used. She shivered as quatrains, sonnets, and limericks were stuffed inside. By the end of a single afternoon she was like a noticeboard crammed with fleshy post-it notes, and a silent noticeboard at that. She died that same night–maybe of septicemia, or simple blood-loss, but most likely asphyxia. I doubt her heaving ribs could take the weight of all that wet, overlapping skin.

The touching aspect was the way her son–fourteen-year-old Harry–offered himself afterwards. And when Harry died, his example inspired the entire street to even greater endeavors. Not just longer poems but sharper, deeper scribing knives. Rank on rank, the residents of

Inkerman Street learned to stand like sentinels, soundlessly resolute, butchering themselves and each other with exquisite care.

***

Today is my ninety-fifth birthday. Nothing special about that, and I'd normally be spending it alone with my journals, but no... on this occasion my neighbours are celebrating with me. A note was posted through my letterbox yesterday. That in itself is an honor–nowadays all writing is the business strictly of the Tree.

The note was written on crinkly testicular skin, extremely hard to read. Fortunately, it was short:

"Arthur, you are invited to turn up at the Tree today at sunset for a surprise. Don't be late!"

It wasn't a poem, of course. No one writes poetry any longer except to the Tree, and that entirely upon flesh, upon bone and vital organs. The latest batch of children on our street only grasped what I meant by paper when I opened a journal to show them.

I dressed for the occasion: my soft moccasins, and my best brown corduroy jacket.

I assumed other people would be dressed normally, and swelled with pride when I saw that no, they had also come decked out in their finest. All the houses on Inkerman Street were overcrowded these days, fifty to a room at least, everyone wanting deeper intimacy with their own and each other's skin, but I swear almost all of them had stopped making love and versifying to come out to see me.

It was humbling. People jostled shoulders, creating space, everyone shuffling aside. A makeshift corridor was formed between the queues, so I could totter my way in a fairly straight line to the Tree. I'd barely seen its lower boughs in years due to the sheer numbers of people lining my window ledges, but today, those window ledges and even some doorways were clear.

Hands reached out to remove my corduroy jacket, and the gentleness of the act moved me to tears. My black cotton socks and moccasins followed. I barely felt the moment a woman tugged my briefs off. Hoisted on dozens of shoulders, I was raised by strong male and female lovers up the branches.

Everything took place in utter silence except for the slide of bodies. I gazed up, astonished to see so many people in the Magnolia Tree. They crouched, sat, or stood. The Tree, over five hundred feet tall now, could easily take their weight.

Children adorned the canopy, the only residents light enough to rest in the upper fringe. To do so, they'd starved themselves, of course, as had I. I barely weighed anything now. A note had been dropped on my doormat five months ago, simply saying 'The thinnest verse is purest.' I intuited its meaning at once: *Famish yourself.*

That famishment now allowed me to reach the very zenith of the Tree. Passed up on the stick-arms and dying last breaths of children, I found my wasted body draped across the canopy like a sacrament. I even had a seat–a cradle knitted by six lesbians from the wombs of their dead lovers.

Not wanting to keep anyone waiting, I settled my scrawny backside inside.

Goodness, I was a long way up–way, way up. From here, I could see the entire city. I hadn't left the street for quite a while–years and years, actually. There was so much dead skin permanently flaking like confetti off the Magnolia that I hadn't needed to shop. The Tree provided, once we restricted our appetites to appropriately biblical levels of malnourishment.

I'd been luckier than some on that front. I'd had the journals to nibble. No one fought me over them. Paper set against skin? That didn't cut it these days. Anyway, as decent as the early paper odes, verses, and rhymes had been, they were amateurish demonstrations of fealty compared to what we were stripping off our bodies now.

Even so, as I gazed broadly over the city from my high perch, what I saw shocked me. The metropolis was gone. Where there had been buildings and streets, they were mostly turned to rubble, except for a dozen or so areas like ours, each with its own towering Magnolia Tree.

I was still admiring the incredible view when the toddlers below me began a painful scratching at my wrists and ankles. They knew their business–loosening skin away from the tendons was second nature to them these days. My knackered-out flesh was also flimsy already, so it didn't take them long. A second group of youngsters began stripping the dry skin from the edges of my scalp. A third group, with specially sharpened fingernails, bent forward like cherubs over my navel. I could see the inspiration in their eyes as they sliced expertly into it, fashioning an inkwell from my bellybutton. One of them, slightly older than the others, dipped a finger in the blood pooling inside and asked me gently, 'What do you want to write?'

It was such a privilege–to have someone else do it, I mean, rather than write the sacrifice yourself–that for a moment I couldn't speak. Also, imbecilically, I hadn't thought in advance about what I wanted to say, and try as I might, I couldn't come up with anything appropriate– not a single true, fragile emotion.

To hide my shame from the boy, I pretended to have a cough.

The children scratched away. What was being done

to me today represented an honor so deep that I had no comparison for it. Unable to find any words, I smiled at the closest boy, then lost his face in the general deluge of pain. They were peeling me, I realised. The agony gave me an excuse to utter incoherent sounds which I tried, not very successfully, to rhyme.

The boy hanging over my navel hastily wrote. He followed my lips, guessing at my intentions.

The skin around my eyes had been puffy for years. Two boys tore it away, while three girls fought over the red strips of my nostrils. Hurriedly, while I still could, I gazed over the panorama of the city.

It was a beautiful sight. So orderly–filled with such well-behaved lines. Thousands, no, hundreds of thousands of acolytes, perhaps millions, all silently queuing around the Magnolia Trees. The citizenry went mostly naked now. Many were scarred head to foot in brown crusts. They were the wounds of love, but from this distance, with my fading vision I must say, the people looked less like prayerful souls and more like walking strips of beef jerky. Some were more lucent than the others, the sunset flashing artfully off their moist, recently delivered flesh.

Quickly, before my eyeballs were blinded by writing, I peered between the branches of our own street's Magnolia. It wasn't the tallest of the trees in the city, but to my admittedly biased sight, it seemed the most venerable, the thickest set, certainly the oldest. And what I saw out there, beyond its hinterland, was awe-inspiring. Famished, brave young men and women across the city were outdoing each other. The best serving I could dish up to the Magnolia Tree in my final hour was a purulence of worn, abraded, liver-worted flesh. These young paladins were holding out skin-strips tauter than the dreams of athletes. Several bore sections of muscle taken from their backs so hefty that they could barely raise them up in their weakened state, but nevertheless they did so, lifting the pulsing flesh high to the tree in proof of how much they cared.

And from up here, where the sound traveled well in the silences of the city, it wasn't quite silent after all. Many out there were whispering: lively poems, livelier breaths. Words querulous, lacerated from torn throats. Quiet verses of love.

END

OTHER HELLBOUND BOOKS
www.hellboundbooks.com

PEDE:

An affectionate homage to the creature feature! The once luxurious Mountainview Spa Hotel in the heart of California's Coachella valley lies decaying, abandoned and heavily boarded up - the site of a radioactive, "dirty" bomb explosion five years' previously. Zoology Professor, Jane Lucas, harbors a lifelong phobia of *Scolopendra gigantea,* the Giant Centipede, despite being the world's leading authority on the creature. Following the savage deaths of two teenagers who broke into the hotel to cavort in the natural underground spa and the discovery of centipede remains almost three times natural size, the professor teams up with four of her students to investigate.

Their expedition soon becomes a fight for survival when they're trapped inside the hotel with a gang of violent thugs and a voracious swarm of oversized centipedes that infest the place - and then discover another creature even more terrifying is hunting in the Mountainview's deserted hallways: a centipede of impossibly monstrous proportions... ravenous and desperate to feed.

Anthology of Splatterpunk 2

splat·ter·punk
noun
informal
noun: splatterpunk

Definition: "A literary genre characterized by graphically described scenes of an extremely gory nature."

Welcome once again, fellow gore lovers, to HellBound Books' second foray into the deliciously bloody, innards-strewn world of splatterpunk!

Death, dismemberment, and destruction abound within these pages, as we bring to you nineteen perfectly ghoulish tales of terror that are definitely not to be read while eating!

Go on, we dare you!

You have short tales from: Shannon Blake Skelton, Juan Ozuna, Sarah Moon, Seaton Kay-Smith, S.C. Vincent, S. Michael Wilson, Carson Demmans, Diana Parrilla, Michael Errol Swaim, John Schlimm, P.J. Verfall, Karly Foland, W.L. Lewis, Caleb James K., Brian J. Smith, D.J. Tuskmor, Terry Grimwood, Dave Davis, and Paul Allih.

Satan Rides Your Daughter Again

In our spine-chilling homage to the late, great Dennis Wheatley and the inimitable Hammer Horror films spawned from his works, HellBound Books presents twenty superlatively satanic stories guaranteed to have you fearing for your very soul?

A whole host of Hell's denizens skulk within these pages, waiting with growing impatience for brave of heart - or the relentlessly foolhardy - to make their otherworldly acquaintance, so please, do venture inside.

If you dare?

Featuring hellish tales from: L. G. Merrick, Henry Myllylä, Alan Derosby, A.K. McCarthy, Brian James Lewis, C. C. Parker, Chisto Healy, Leo J. Winters, R.C. Mulhare, Henry Myllylä, J.B. Toner, Glen Damien Campbell, Nathan Blake, Gerald Dean Rice, Ricki Whatley, Carlton Herzog, Len M. Ruth, Vivian Kasley, Carson Demmans, Mark Towse, and Alexander Marai.

Suburban Nightmares

Welcome to the 'burbs!

We're just a short commute from the hustle and bustle of the big city. We know you'll just love the peaceful, gated communities where smiling children ride their bikes safely in the street and neighbors invite everyone to their backyard barbecues....
But pay no mind to that shadow you thought you saw running between the well-manicured lawns while a happy husband dines on homemade meatloaf with his lovely young family after a long, hard day at the office. And those screams you heard drowning out the sounds of his middle-aged neighbor washing his beloved red sports car on the weekends?
Ignore them.
After all, you're completely safe here in the 'burbs...
HellBound Books brings together 24 phenomenal writers to spin you such disturbing, grisly tales of murder and monsters and all things horror, all slap-bang in the middle of that beautiful, protected suburban life.
Featuring some of the very best independent horror authors writing today: Adam Carlson, Alayna Frankenberry, Braden Benzinger, Danni Bowen, Adam Carlson, Dave Davis, Carson Demmans, Ryan Dyer, Alayna Frankenberry, Terry Grimwood, Bryan Holm, Jade Jiao, Paul Lonardo, Alexander Marais, Shannon Mills, Shawn Montgomery, Jason Moore, Tilsen Mulalley, Renee Mulhare, HP Newquist, Damon Nomad, Matthew Piskun, Colin Adams-Toomey, Julie Aaron, and Steve Zisson

Anthology of Horror

hor·ror
/'hôrər/

A literary or film genre concerned with arousing feelings of horror.

Rest assured, HellBound Books knows what scares you!

Skulking around in the deepest, thickest, darkest shadows of our authors' imaginations lies a whole host of terrifying tales to scare you witless and stir your greatest fears and, dear reader, we have compiled twenty-one such short stories for that specific purpose within the beautifully crafted pages of this very tome!

So, dig in – we dare you – and do remember to leave a light on…

Featuring short tales of terror from: Cory Andrews, Kathrin Classen, William Presley, John Schlimm. K.L. Lord, Jane Nightshade, K. John O'Leary, Dante Bilec, D. H. Parish, Whitney McShan, Keiran Meeks, Josh Darling, Paul Lonardo, Martyn Lawrence, Eric J. Juneau, Terry Campbell, Brett King, Sophia Cauduro, Christina Meeks, Kody Greene, and HellBound Books' very own James H Longmore.

A HellBound Books Publishing LLC Publication

www.hellboundbookspublishing.com

www.ingramcontent.com/pod-product-compliance
Lightning Source LLC
Chambersburg PA
CBHW020759310726
48969CB00002B/611